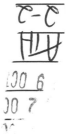

He'd done okay today, thanks mostly to Bonnie, but how to live with the crushing guilt of his delay in response?

It had happened in his first emergency after Clara died. His colleagues had told him it was only natural, to give himself time, but he'd backed away in horror. A man not to be trusted. A doctor unable to deal with emergencies. A man ashamed of a vocation that had been his life.

So he had run to Bali.

Avoided any contact with medicine. And drifted. Drifted until a determined little midwife had dragged him into the very situation he'd been running from...

Dear Reader

I was fortunate enough to visit Bali earlier this year with a friend—another midwife—and we savoured the Balinese kindness and genuine pride in their customs and country. We rode bicycles down a volcano, attended Balinese cooking classes, visited the Bumi Sehat Birth Centre in Ubud, and learnt some of the customs around birth and childhood in Bali.

I really wanted to share some of the joy of these wonderful people, and so does my hero Harry St Clair—a man hiding from himself in Bali.

In March I visited Alice Springs, Kings Canyon and Ayers Rock with my middle son Andrew. We hired an off-road vehicle and hit the red dust with a vengeance. Luckily he's a diesel mechanic, and fixed that flat tyre in no time. I just kept typing. The scenery and the sky and the vast distances were awe-inspiring.

Enter Bonnie McKenzie, midwife and Outback community nurse, who's flown up to Bali from Darwin on a brief holiday. Bonnie is a straight-talker, not in the market for a man, but even she can see there's simmering sensual tension under the surface when she meets Harry. As for Harry—he doesn't know what's hit him.

When Bonnie leaves for Central Australia a week later Harry has to follow. Maybe he could just dip his toe in the real world again? But Ayers Rock and the rugged Australian Outback don't believe in half-measures, and in all its stark beauty the red centre does the rest. Welcome to Harry and Bonnie's world.

Warmest wishes for your trip in the Outback!

Fiona

HARRY ST CLAIR: ROGUE OR DOCTOR?

BY
FIONA McARTHUR

MILLS & BOON

First published in Great Britain 2011
by Mills & Boon, an imprint of Harlequin (UK) Limited.
Large Print edition 2011
Harlequin (UK) Limited, Eton House,
18-24 Paradise Road, Richmond, Surrey TW9 1SR

© Fiona McArthur 2011

ISBN: 978 0 263 21781 0

Printed and bound in Great Britain
by CPI Antony Rowe, Chippenham, Wiltshire

A mother to five sons, **Fiona McArthur** is an Australian midwife who loves to write. Medical™ Romance gives Fiona the scope to write about all the wonderful aspects of adventure, romance, medicine and midwifery that she feels so passionate about—as well as an excuse to travel! Now that her boys are older, Fiona and her husband Ian are off to meet new people, see new places, and have wonderful adventures. Fiona's website is at www.fionamcarthur.com

Recent titles by the same author:

MIDWIFE, MOTHER…ITALIAN'S WIFE*
MIDWIFE IN THE FAMILY WAY*
THE MIDWIFE AND THE MILLIONAIRE
MIDWIFE IN A MILLION

Lyrebird Lake Maternity

Praise for Fiona McArthur and her fabulous *Lyrebird Lake Maternity* mini-series:

'Ms McArthur has created a series
that is powerfully moving and yet filled with
characters that could be any other member of
your family because they're down-to-earth
people who are just human like everyone else.
Thank you, Ms McArthur,
for a thoroughly enjoyable time spent
in your world of Lyrebird Lake.'
—*Cataromance.com*

To Lesley, who makes me smile,
Vicki, who smiles as well,
and Margo, from all those years ago.

All friends who shared Bali with me.

And my son, Andrew, who changed that tyre
in the desert on the way to Ayers Rock and
shared the magic of the red centre with me.

And always Ian, my own rock.
Happy thirtieth anniversary, my love.

CHAPTER ONE

SUNSET. Glorious Bali Island.

Harry St Clair glanced around the hotel swimming pool and grimaced. His usual calm deserted him just thinking of going back to Australia and the practice of medicine. To make it worse he was half an hour early to tell them it wasn't happening.

The pool chairs were littered with tourists sipping cocktails while waiting for sunset and he was careful not to catch the eye of any of them, especially the women, as he scanned for the man who'd arranged to meet him. Now was not the time for dalliance.

Bonnie McKenzie watched him arrive. All the women did. When he approached the pool the ladies' necks stretched like those of inquisitive turtles to follow his broad shoulders, and she rolled her eyes. She could hear Sacha, in the chair next to her, whisper to Jacinta, and she hoped the words didn't carry to where he stood.

'They call him the package. 'Cause he looks good, talks good and I'll bet my new black bikini he feels good. But he's a heartbreaker. Tells all the women he's not into relationships.' Jacinta sighed dreamily as her friend went on. 'He's not staying at the hotel. I asked the waitress. He's here to see someone.'

To Bonnie the man didn't look like a package. He looked like an isolated lighthouse off the coast of Wales that she'd once seen on television.

Alone, surrounded by jagged rocks, immovable in any storm as he waited, protected by a wall of sceptical disinterest in everyone until an older woman in a ceremonial sarong tapped him on the arm and he smiled. Then everything changed.

Then there was something about the tilt of his head and warm greeting as he responded to the Balinese lady with such kindness, such honest charm, it called even to Bonnie—which surprised her, because since selling her engagement ring she'd vowed she'd never be that receptive to a man again.

Good genes, her gran would have said. Bonnie found herself thinking, *Good jeans*, and she looked away and pressed her lips together to hold the smile in. These young midwives she'd travelled with from Darwin were a bad influence.

She looked back, fairly sure he couldn't see her under the shadow of her umbrella'd deckchair. He was talking to a man now, shaking his head at the elderly sunburnt tourist she'd seen around the hotel, but her eyes were drawn back to the younger one.

There, good lighthouse, a beam of radiance as the man beside him made him smile, and again, when he lifted one strong hand and shook the other man's hand. So he could soften and, yes, Bonnie could see why the girls felt the need to discuss him.

Now he looked casual and relaxed, lazily footloose in his cut-off blue jeans, his long brown legs testament to some sporting pursuit that kept him fit. Being footloose and declaring it seemed imminently sensible for him, and much better than stomping on hearts to scale the heights of a profession, like some Bonnie knew.

She could see this man's loosely buttoned sports shirt fought a losing battle if it wanted to disguise the width of his shoulders or the leanly muscular biceps that peeked out of the short sleeves. Not something that usually fascinated her, leanly muscular men, but those arms teased her now, corded with strength and generous with leashed power. She glanced down at the sudden swish of goose bumps across her own skin and lifted her face to find the breeze that caused it.

Hopefully there was a breeze…

Bonnie shifted back further under the umbrella in case her malady was too much sun. She glanced around and saw she wasn't the only woman still sneaking a peek. So, thankfully, she wasn't the only basket case because it seemed he called to every person with two X chromosomes.

No doubt being such a woman magnet could be a trial for him after a while and she wasn't about to join the party.

The thought settled her. Good. At least she had her common sense back, though she had to admit there was something shadowed and intriguing in his persona that begged the question of his past. Well, there was stuff in her own past, plenty of baggage for the unwary, and he could keep his load because she had enough of her own.

Bonnie looked away to the reds and golds of the Balinese sunset leaking colour into the waves. When Sacha actually nudged her to admire him again, Bonnie shook her head and whispered, 'Not interested in packages. I'm here to enjoy the sunset without discussing men.'

Sacha rolled her eyes. 'As you like. You watch the pretty ball in the sky and I'll watch my own view.' The girl winked and Bonnie shook her head and pressed her lips together again. She had to. The incorrigible young midwives had been making her smile since she'd unexpectedly joined their holiday.

Pushed into a short vacation by her friends in Darwin, this break had been designed to put a spring back in Bonnie's step before she started the new job at Ayers Rock, or Uluru now, she reminded herself, the ancient Aboriginal name for their sacred place. And, in fact, although her mouth still felt a bit stiff, she was finding more to smile about every day.

The last sliver of molten fire disappeared into the sea with an audible sigh, though, strictly speaking, the noise came from the collective breath of appreciation from the watchers as they turned and began to meander back to their rooms before the tropical night encroached.

'So what are we doing for dinner?' The girls lived for action and Bonnie searched in her head for a skerrick of enthusiasm. Nope. None there.

She'd floated quietly in the deep end of the pool last night and avoided them because she'd spent the first three days with a plastered-on smile. Now she just wanted to soak in the calmness that she had to admit had unexpectedly filtered back into her soul by Balinese osmosis.

'Think I might curl up on one of the lounges and stare at the colours as they fade. Then maybe dinner in my room.'

'Okay.' The girls jumped up now. The nature show was over and youth needed diversion. 'Maybe we'll catch up with you later at the club.' They grinned, waved and took off like they'd miss the chance of a lifetime if they didn't run.

Harry St Clair watched the scantily clad nymphs hurry away but his eyes were drawn back to the quietly restful woman in the chair. He'd noticed her while he'd been talking to Bob. Allowed himself to be distracted from Bob's attempt at persuasion, though it hadn't been a hardship scoping her out. And here he was, still loitering when he could have gone.

He hesitated, conscious of his own aversion to disruption by people when he wished to be alone, and very aware of the 'don't bother me' signals that flew above her like those Balinese kites you'd see any afternoon here—happy doing their own thing.

But she intrigued him, attracted him ridiculously with a little flick of her hair and the stretch of her fingers when she put her glass down, and suddenly he didn't want to eat dinner in peace.

A little harmless weather conversation with an intriguing little sun-lover would chase away the demons the job offer had left him with. And he'd had a beer already so he wasn't driving back to Ubud until tomorrow.

She looked nothing like the usual women he flirted with. She looked more like someone he'd actually converse with. Like his housekeeper's sister, he'd just seen, or any woman safely married and motherly and therefore not interested in him as a fling, but this young woman seemed someone he could briefly connect with, which in itself was strange. Connection hadn't been on his agenda—especially in the last two years.

Serene, that was what she was, though serenity over sadness? Maybe it was just his ego because she hadn't looked his way at all and she obviously didn't feel any of the vibes he was getting.

Harry gave up the struggle and crossed to her umbrella. 'I wondered if they'd leave you alone,' he said, and as an opening remark it was pretty lame, but she looked even better up close. He was right. Her eyes did hold a background of darkness, or maybe green-toned memories that made him want to ask why. Maybe that was why he'd felt drawn to her.

She wore a cheap silk dress that looked incredibly cute on her, unlike the flaunting swimwear the others had worn, as if she wasn't confident displaying her body.

Shame, that.

The concept of conversation grew even more attractive. If he could convince her, that was, because she looked like he was the last person she needed to see, and usually that was enough deterrent when he just didn't care enough.

She took her time to tilt her firm little chin to a ridiculous angle so she could look up at his face. 'Actually, they're my friends.'

'Sorry. Didn't mean to be rude.'

Bonnie was in a dilemma. The palpitations had come from nowhere and his proximity was making it hard not to blush. The lighthouse offered her the five-star smile free of charge. Dazzling sweep of light. Then his words sank in. And even an apology. Not something Bonnie was used to getting from men. Nice of him, Bonnie thought, but she wished he hadn't because she didn't need more reasons to be attracted.

'I'm not judging,' he said. 'I remember being young.'

In years he was nowhere near old but there was a wealth of experience, possibly not all good, behind those dazzling eyes of his. Some days she felt decrepit too but didn't know this guy well enough to agree.

'Poor you.' Though he didn't look poor in any sense of the word. She wondered what had happened to make him feel aged but that was probably all part of his pick-up plan. He had to be somewhere between thirty and thirty-five, which put him five years older than her at least.

Up close he was even more impressive in a gut-wrenching, tear-the-breath-from-your-throat kind of way she didn't like to admit, but thankfully she could now call on months of training in unattainability. 'Do I know you?'

More smile and the look he was giving suggested he'd like to move that way. She ignored the little buzz that grew with the idea. 'I don't know. Do you?' He held out one tanned hand and she looked at it. 'Harry St Clair,' she heard him say.

Such beautiful hands. Long fingers, square-clipped nails, fine hairs across a strong back—and a wedding band. She hadn't noticed that before and she didn't know why she'd be shocked. Maybe because the way he was smiling at her had nothing to do with fidelity. It was a strange old world when people could act like this.

Bonnie uncurled herself from the chair and stood up next to him. She was tall but he was taller by a fair margin and that only made her more annoyed. She couldn't hide the contempt in her eyes but then, that was what happened when you smelled a rat when you expected aftershave.

She raised her eyebrows and then her chin. 'I don't know you.' She shook her head. 'Do I know your wife?'

His hand dropped and his other came over the ring and hid it from view. 'I doubt that. She's been gone for more than two years.'

Bonnie closed her eyes. He was a widower? Hell. 'I'm sorry.' But it was too late now. She'd jumped to the conclusion he was just like Jeremy, Dr Sleaze, with the harem of women in the wings and their joint bank account he'd emptied.

Infidelity brought back the memories she'd thought she'd zippered away in a sealed compartment, like she'd packed her suitcase to fly into Denpasar. But that was no excuse for accusing him.

She could feel her fingers against her side, twitching a little as if hoping he'd put his hand out again and give her another shot. But her hand wouldn't make the journey by itself. Her barriers were secure. That was a good thing. 'I'm sorry. I have to go.'

Harry wasn't ready for that. Hadn't expected it because it didn't happen to him often. In fact, he couldn't remember the last time he'd been given the flick so smoothly. He followed her. 'I didn't catch your name.'

She kept walking and obviously she didn't care if he heard her or not. 'I didn't throw it,' she muttered.

So this was how it felt, Harry reminded himself. Unpleasant, but more interesting. Maybe he was a masochist? The wall around her was higher than the one around the Royal Palace in Ubud and twice as fascinating. He knew all about walls to keep people out. Suddenly it became imperative he have more than a brief chat with her about the weather.

He took two big steps and caught up with her. 'But you threw an insult. I'm only looking for a nice platonic dinner partner to share Jimbaran Bay with. Maybe we could talk about that?'

At least she'd stopped. Turned to look at him. But she wasn't saying anything. He could feel those liquid eyes assessing him, and he felt as if he were posing, like in a passport photograph, with that frozen, trying-not-to-look-like-a-psychopath expression on his face.

It was as if she didn't know what to say so she didn't say anything at all. More people should try that. It was attractive. And at least it wasn't no.

He went on because he knew he had seconds before she disappeared. Make it count, old boy. 'I really am Harry St Clair. They know me here. I'm reluctant to ask someone else.' He glanced around as if there were loads of women he could ask. 'All those candles and tables in the sand at Jimbaran are just too romantic.' He shrugged. 'I can tell you loathe me. I'd feel safe with you.'

He felt like groaning. What the heck was falling

out of his mouth? He was an idiot and he wouldn't blame her if she ran away. Where had that come from?

'I think you've tickets on yourself,' she said, and her eyes suddenly looked as lush as the local jungle and just as dangerous. Maybe this wasn't such a good idea because this woman had weapons he wasn't that sure he could hold out against if she used them all.

'I apologise. I was insensitive about your wife.' She looked away and he thought he heard her sigh. 'I don't know you enough to loathe you but I guess I could think about trying.'

Bonnie glanced over her shoulder at the pinking horizon. Was she mad? Was it too late to squirm out? 'The sun's gone. Why go to Jimbaran now?' She'd heard of the bay past the airport. 'Everything I've heard's about the sunset.'

He slanted a quick look at her as he followed her towards the main building of the resort. 'I enjoy eating seafood on the beach. But not alone. My treat?'

'Wow. A big spender. I might choose lobster.' Even to her it sounded like a yes. She didn't know the man. But then, the girls had implied he wasn't a serial killer. Most men who looked like him usually weren't. No doubt some women would do their own dying to attract his attention.

But there was that tiny worrying buzz that hummed somewhere near her stomach when she looked at him. The last time she'd been attracted this noticeably to a man it had ended in major disaster and she'd decided she truly enjoyed being single.

Which would be why her friends had practically forced her onto the plane to Denpasar. Hmm. Maybe she didn't enjoy total isolation from all men all the time. Maybe she just needed a holiday flirtation to restore her self-esteem and a sense of balance?

'I'm good for the bill.' He glanced at his watch, a flash one, and she wondered if it was real or one of the ten-dollar fakes that were sold on every corner in Kuta. It looked real but then, so did he and she didn't believe in him. And this hotel was nice but not expensive. Not a place for watches like his. Lots of things didn't make sense.

He went on. 'I'm starving. You look great. Don't suppose you'd come as you are?'

He was way too pushy but she was hungry now, not sure where that appetite had come from. She glanced down at the halter-necked silk dress she'd picked up at the markets. It was cool, comfortable and matched the sequined slides she'd bought with it. Why change for a man she barely knew?

'I'll leave a note under the girls' door.' It didn't hurt to pretend somebody cared where she went and with whom.

He nodded. 'Great idea. In case we're late.'

Cool green eyes met blue. 'We won't be late.'

Harry looked across at her and tried to figure it out. Every time he looked into her eyes he fell more deeply under her spell. And she was determined. It was her way or the highway and he respected that. But it would be good to settle why he'd been so affected by her and then get her out of his head. Note to self: not into his bed. Good plan.

Harry hoped she couldn't see how amazed he was she'd agreed at all. He'd thought they'd imploded after she'd mentioned Clara but they'd come around again. He was ridiculously pleased about that. Maybe it was just the fact he could talk to her and not feel he had to be someone he wasn't. Not sure why that was either.

'I'll get a taxi, then, shall I?'

CHAPTER TWO

IT SEEMED Jimbaran Bay had become an institution like Kuta with a long strip of restaurants.

The beach lay stretched to the north of them with choose-your-fish and lobster tanks, flame-leaping barbecues and the biggest array of fresh seafood Bonnie had seen for years.

Then there were the hundreds of wooden tables spread across the sand almost down to the lapping water, each restaurant's tables abutting each other as they squeezed side by side.

A pall of barbecue smoke lay over the parking area when the taxi dropped them off, people coming and going, taxis and private cars and even limousines jostling for space. And, of course, hundreds of motorbikes parked in orderly rows.

Bonnie gazed in awe at the confusion and

choice. 'How do you know which restaurant to eat in?'

'Been before. I have my favourite and they'll save a good table for me.' Harry watched her drink it in. Her pleasure made him look again, inhale the smoke, hear the chatter between the competing restaurants, and recognise some of the reasons he seemed to end up here when he came down to this end of Bali.

But most of his unusual lightness of heart seemed to be emanating from being with the woman at his side. Strange, that.

She walked with him down the concrete passage between two vying shopfronts and he could feel her presence near his hip like a little force-field of energy reacting with him. Swirls of awareness prickled like the sprays of loose sand that flicked off their shoes as they walked.

When they hit the beach the sun had well and truly gone, a darkening silhouette of a fishing boat glided out on the waves as the candles flared into life along the tables. Darkness fell softly, like one of those cashmere pashminas the women wore here. He heard her sigh out a little more tension from those militant shoulders and it made him feel good.

Bonnie felt herself relax as she looked around. This was different. Time out of the real world, maybe because of the semidarkness. She could get used to eating in the dark on a beach too. It was so unlike her to come with a stranger but there were enough people to keep her safe here and she could always catch her own taxi home. And suddenly it felt fun to be out with a good-looking man for an uncomplicated dinner. Her friends would be very proud of her.

They crunched through the sand all the way down to the water's edge. Bonnie glanced at couples and families and noisy groups of tourists all munching and laughing in groups as they passed.

To her delight every table had at least one person sucking milk from a coconut through a straw. The cheerful mood lifted her spirits even higher. She used to be a happy person and it was nice to glimpse a little joy again.

Finally their waiter stopped at a table. It wasn't quite in the water but there was no one in front to obscure the last of the glow on the horizon. She stood for a moment and just gazed out over the waves. Definitely a cool place to have dinner.

Harry beat the waiter to her chair and pulled it out for her. 'Your throne, madam.'

She could feel the hairs on her arms respond to his nearness. Visceral response. Pheromones. This wasn't good. She wanted flirtation, not irreversible fascination. Please, not that sort of happy. Her eyes met his and she didn't smile. 'I'm your dinner partner, not your date.'

Snap. Reality bit. Harry was silent as he sat down and then picked up his fork to examine it. Carefully—while he let her words sink in. Nice fork. Silver with three tines. Not much of interest there. 'Got it. No chairs held. And I'll have no deep and meaningful conversations from you either,' he joked, but there was an underlying truth in his words.

He glanced up and caught the fiercely guarded expression on her face. She was as bad as him. Funny how he'd never realised how bad he was. 'What about car doors? Did that offend you?' He saw her face tighten even more.

She closed her eyes and held up her hands and he could foresee the moment when she'd say she shouldn't have come.

Panic flared in her eyes and he cursed his stupidity.

Some bloke had done a doozy on her. Oops, he thought, but didn't say it out loud. He accepted the message and tapped the table so she looked at him. He tried selling his smile again. 'I'm sorry.'

That was when he realised he didn't know her name. Pleasant and non-threatening dinner conversation coming up. 'I really don't want to eat alone. But what shall I call you?'

Bonnie forced herself to calm down. Panic weakened defences and that was the last thing she wanted. Her name? Now, there was a dilemma. She had this stupid urge to make up a name, something wildly outrageous that he'd know wasn't real, so it didn't cause problems but would maintain distance in case she needed more space than he was willing to give.

Brain vacuum didn't help. 'Bonnie.'

'So tell me, Bonnie…' He paused and she smiled to herself because it was plain he didn't believe that really was her name. Delicious.

'Are you in Bali long?' He sat back in his chair with a little smile curving his lips. Good grief, he had gorgeous lips.

She blinked. 'A week. Then I start a new job.'

'So what's your new job?' When he leaned back his shirt stretched over his chest and her mouth dried.

She tried to unobtrusively rustle up some saliva so she could answer. 'Outreach nursing, at Ayers Rock. I'm a registered nurse and midwife and do short stints in isolated places.'

A strange expression crossed his face so fast

she couldn't guess the cause. Interesting but he didn't explain it. Just nodded.

Blimey. Talk about danger, Harry thought. The same place as the job he'd declined. And too close to a town he wanted to forget. His wife had been a midwife, they'd met at Katherine when he'd worked for the RFDS. Fate was out to smack him apparently.

When he changed the subject she didn't seem to notice. Thank goodness. He'd already said he only wanted a dinner partner, which apparently suited her fine.

Back to discussing her might be safer. 'So what have you done here in paradise you wouldn't have done at home?'

She gestured to the beach in front of them. 'Apart from dining with a man I don't know, you mean?'

He wasn't silly enough to fall into the trap. 'Hmm.'

She shrugged. 'Nothing, really. Swam, but I did that in Darwin, shopped at markets and watched the sunset over the ocean, but we do that at Mindil on Thursdays and Sundays in Darwin too.'

He watched her think about it. Her thoughts may as well have been typed up on a screen. It was amusing how transparent she was and he found it delightfully refreshing. 'While I'm here I'd like to see some of the countryside. The terraced rice fields and a volcano—none of those where I come from.'

He nodded. He'd found a topic. 'So you should do the bike ride from Agung.'

He could tell she'd vaguely heard of it but couldn't place it. 'And that would be…?'

He gestured loosely in the direction of Kuta. 'Up in the mountains, a couple of hours' drive, well worth it. The bike ride's about twenty-five kilometres long.'

'Probably not happening, then.' She shrugged. 'I haven't ridden a bike for ten years.' She laughed at the thought. 'That'd be a sight. I wouldn't be able to stand up after.'

Bonnie tried not to get sucked under his spell but his smile was infecting her. Flashing like a beam over the waves when she least expected to see it in the gloom and made her think of the lighthouse again. He sat forward a little, leaning towards her in an effort to enthuse her. 'The ride's all downhill. Through villages, rice fields, over a river. You'd love it.'

She only had a few days left. She doubted she'd organise herself enough for that. 'I don't think bike riding's on my list.'

She watched him frown. 'Sure it is. If you're up for it, let me know. I have great contacts.'

She'd love it but she didn't need his help. Or his company. One night of exposure and flirtation was enough to start with and this guy was just too potent for a bruised heart like hers. 'I'll see what the girls say.' They'd probably ask how many men were going. But she wasn't debunking the myth that she had protection.

Thankfully it seemed he'd accepted she

wouldn't be pinned to a decision. 'So what else would you like to do while on beautiful Bali?'

Well, she knew she didn't want to talk about herself. Never had really. 'How about you tell me what you're going to do. How long you're here for?'

He raised his dark brows and smiled. 'So bossy,' he said. She wished.

Then, as if vaguely surprised at himself, he did answer her. 'I'm here indefinitely. There's a house up in Ubud. My mother lived there a few months every year. I've been visiting for a while.'

Real watch evidently. 'Wow. And I'm guessing you have servants and everything.' Even she could hear the reverse snobbery in her voice. Where had that come from?

He tilted his head and she guessed he'd heard it too. 'There's a family that maintain the buildings, yes. Have done for fifty years. Ketut and his wife have looked after my mother and she looked after them. But like family—not servants. You have a problem with that?'

Of course she didn't. And the idea of extra family was a sweet one. She'd be happy to have a distant aunt, let alone a Balinese family looking after her. No reason on earth why she should mind except to wonder why he wanted to waste his time with her. 'No. I'm sorry. I keep putting my foot in it with you—not sure why. It's not common for me.'

'Maybe it's because I keep you off balance.' He grinned. 'But, then, that's not nice for a platonic friend so I'll apologise too.' He glanced down at the menu. 'We'd better order before it's too dark for you to see what you're eating.'

Now her hunger seemed to have soaked into the sand under her feet and she wished she could follow it. Who was out of practice as a relaxed dinner companion? 'What are you having?'

He put the menu back on the table. 'I'll do the set plate with lots of seafood and a side salad.'

She couldn't even read the menu in the dark. 'Sounds good.'

He sat straighter and glanced around. 'You get

a drink with it. Have you tried the local beer? It's very light.'

She'd seen it advertised everywhere. 'No, but bought the T-shirt.'

He grinned and signalled the waiter, who appeared like magic. 'We'll have two Jimbaran specials, two beers and a coconut drink, please.'

Obviously she'd been blatant with her curiosity about the coconuts. But it was nice he'd seen her interest. Or was it? She'd need to watch this man. He was unobtrusively delightful.

The waiter produced two beers from his passing friend, set them down and departed with a big white smile. Harry handed one over to her. Then he carried on the conversation as if there'd been no break.

'Those T-shirts are the most common exports with tourists. Hope you didn't pay more than twenty thousand rupees for it.'

So he was focused. She'd need to watch that too, but she'd been dying to talk to someone about this.

She tapped her glass with her fingernail. 'I have issues with bartering. I can see the Balinese enjoy it, but I'd prefer just to buy the darn thing without the hassle. I find it very stressful to pretend I'm offended at the price.'

He took a sip and when he didn't answer, she decided to copy him. A tentative sip. The drink was light, still beery and she wasn't that much of a fan, but it was cold and wet and felt wonderful going down.

Then he said, 'Wimp,' and she nearly choked. He grinned and went on. 'Barter is fun. It's part of Balinese culture, like mental gymnastics. Good bargaining can make a huge difference to a family wage if they're lucky. But the experience should never be unpleasant or too pushy.'

'Yeah, well. I'm such a sucker.' She sighed. 'What do you do when people look sad and you feel guilty you haven't bought anything?'

'You smile.' He grinned and showed her how. If he smiled at someone like that they'd probably give him the thing, she thought. Free.

He went on. 'It's the secret of Bali. Smile and mean it. For bargaining, if they start at fifty thousand rupees, you offer twenty-five. They'll look horrified, you smile and they'll smile and counter with forty. Then you say thirty and they'll take thirty-five. It's always good to aim for about five thousand under what you want to pay so the seller wins. It's good luck for the seller and we can all do with that.'

Not an accurate picture of barter when she was involved. She tended to wilt at the first horror and fake accusation. 'Forty-nine thousand would be a good barter for me. That sounds easy but it's not.'

The light from the candle flickered across his face. He shook his head and she decided he didn't have a bad angle she could concentrate on. 'That's because you're thinking personal. It's not personal. When it all boils down to it, if you want something, think about what you'd pay for it and be happy. Then change what they're asking into your currency and you'll see you still have a bargain. Carry a printed version of your dollar versus their currency. It's simpler to remember that way.'

She wasn't sure she was ever going to enjoy bargaining but maybe she'd give it a go with a little more enthusiasm. She could write out a conversion table. 'Okay.'

Or maybe she hadn't sounded as convinced as she'd thought because he said, 'Or look for fixed-price shops. There's always one around and then you'll get a fair price, not quite as cheap but they'll take out the wild swings when someone really good reels you in.'

She glanced at his confident face. 'I bet you don't get reeled in.'

'Not often. By the Balinese anyway.' There was an added nuance she didn't want to identify and thankfully their food arrived.

By this time it was darker, and even though her eyes had adjusted, the candle gave off small circles of light that didn't include the platter beside her. The waiter brought two more tiny candlelights but she still couldn't see what she was eating. 'So this is a taste sensation, not a visual one?'

He laughed, deep and amused, and she felt like a trickle of that cool sand under her feet had slid down her back and along her arms. Well, she was on a beach. It was okay. But she had a strong premonition there was more trickling sand to come.

'Want to see your dinner?' She watched him shift his body and reach into his pocket and then suddenly there was a blinding flash.

She rubbed her eyes. He laughed again. 'Sorry. Should've warned you.' His smile beamed in the night as her vision began to recover and he handed her his camera. 'It looks like this.'

Bonnie's meal was captured for posterity and illuminated clearly on the camera screen. 'You're really a do-now-think-later kinda guy, aren't you?' But she could see a long barbecued fish, brown and crunchy, and one gruesome eye. She wished she hadn't seen that but at least she

wouldn't accidentally eat it in the dark. She shuddered.

'The less thinking the better,' he said crypti-
cally, then went on. 'The ones in the shells are
mussels, and despite the thought if you're not
a shellfish eater, they taste wonderful. King
prawns, calamari on skewers, crab and lobster
meat piled on the side. And the green salad.'

It was all recognisable now. Actually, quite a
neat trick to take the photo, she acknowledged,
at least to herself. 'Obviously you've used this in
the dark before.'

He tucked the camera away in his pocket. 'Too
many times on my own. I'm glad you came.'

'So am I.' She was. And feeling more relaxed.
Bonnie didn't think it was the beer, though
maybe it had more of a kick than he was letting
on, but the atmosphere here would make anyone
feel good.

Smiling Balinese waiters, the muted wash
of the waves just a few feet away, candles all
around them and brighter lights in the distance.

Every now and then a plane took off or landed at Ngurah Rai airport across the water and the stars had started to shine more brightly as the night deepened. 'This is pretty cool. Thank you for bringing me.'

'You're welcome.' Her coconut drink arrived and even in the dark it looked huge. 'Do you want me to take a photo of that so you can see it?'

She thought of the brightness of the flash and the disruption of the mood. 'I can guess. It's not worth the eye pain.' She picked it up and the milk inside sloshed. 'I'll never finish this.'

'That's why I only bought one. Drink what you fancy and leave the rest. I'll finish it so you don't feel guilty.'

There was something disturbing about the thought of him drinking from her straw, too easy to picture and not without sensory ramifications. She turned the conversation.

'The stars are amazing.'

'Bit too much light here to do them justice.'

'I love stars but wish I knew more about them.'

'I'm not much better,' he said, and they both glanced up then down at each other and for some reason they both laughed. The beginnings of a dangerous rapport. They both sobered.

Bonnie broke the silence. 'So what do you do while you're over here?' She took a sip and the strong flavour of coconut overlaid the beer.

He attacked his meal as if he wanted distance from that moment too. 'Nothing.'

He paused as if waiting for her to say how terrible to drift between jobs, but she wasn't going to.

For a short time, *nothing* would be great. And that pastime would be as far away from Jeremy as possible. Her ex didn't know anything about cultivating stillness. The longer they were parted the better she was feeling, except she'd learned a very valuable lesson about people who lied.

'So you don't get bored?' She took another bite and chewed while she waited. The fish melted in her mouth and the tang of lime made her sigh with bliss.

He put down his fork. 'Not yet. I do a bit of diving up at Lovina, some surfing.'

She picked up the coconut again. This meal was a symphony of different flavours and she was glad she hadn't chickened out. Surfing, diving, eating on beaches. Sounded idyllic. For a while. 'Do you do anything constructive? What's your profession? Your job when you're not surfing?'

Anything worthwhile? His raised eyebrows noted the observation that lay unspoken between them, but still the question had popped out and mentally she shrugged. Well, she did want to know because surfing and scuba diving wasn't a lifestyle, especially if he was trained to do something useful, or had done in the past.

She'd been devastated by her love life bombing out but she hadn't given up her life to hide in a distant country. No. If she was honest, she'd hidden in work. Which was the reverse of what he'd done, she supposed.

He was silent for a few beats. 'Sometimes I

build things, work in the fields every now and then. And I'm studying yoga.'

The last thing she would have connected with him but then, he did occasionally give off restful vibes. 'I can't quite see you and yoga together.' She thought about it some more. 'So you're going to be a yoga teacher? I guess both our professions are about health.'

'No. I'm studying it for myself.'

She laughed. He amused her, he really did. 'Selfish 'R' Us? Who will look after you if you don't?'

'That's right.' He sat back in his seat and smiled. If she wasn't mistaken, she'd say he was relieved by her amusement.

She couldn't imagine not having work to take her mind off the rest. 'So what about your parents? What do they think of you growing old on an island?'

'They're both dead.'

Oops. 'I'm an orphan too. It sucks.' She really didn't want to talk about this and wasn't sure why she was except she felt somehow responsible for the conversation. 'My mum died when I was twelve. Never knew my father and my gran brought me up. She died three months ago. I nursed her at home.' *And my sleazy fiancé slept with his ex and stole all my money while I was busy.* But she was getting over that. Really.

'Tough, but special. So you normally work as a midwife?'

'Mostly. I trained in Darwin, did a little time in ICU, but mostly a midwife. I love working remote in short stints but you miss out on the births mostly that way.'

She speared another succulent piece of fish. 'And you, before you came here?'

'Different things. None of them useful.' Slam. She felt the whoosh from the shutting door. Now she wished she'd shut her mouth. She kept it closed in case something else came out that she'd regret and ate another piece of fish and left him with the silence. He'd caused it.

Harry had a pretty good idea what she was

thinking. Well, what could he say? She wasn't getting the truth. Oh, did medicine, fell in love, lost wife and child because I was stupid, now have abdicated from world.

By the time she'd finished her fish he could see she was full. Not a big eater, he gathered. In fact, she seemed a little on the thin side.

When the waiter returned he shook his head at the proffered menus. 'I'm guessing you don't need sweets.'

'No, thank you.'

'Any chance of a quick stroll along the beach before we leave?'

She opened her mouth to say no but he kept talking and successfully forestalled her. Another win to him. 'Just to let the food settle. Only as far as the tables go and it's in plain view of everyone.'

He could see she hated the thought of giving in to him again. Her independence amused him and only made him more determined to conquer her reserve. He wanted to win! Now how long since he'd felt that?

Bonnie didn't know where this competitiveness had come from but probably she should listen to it as a warning signal. She was her own woman. Then her mouth said, 'Maybe for a few minutes and then I must get back to my friends.'

'Sure.' He stood up and despite their initial conversation he helped pull out her chair. 'It gets a little tricky in the sand when the chairs sink in a bit.'

Bonnie felt him beside her. Her arms did that hair-waving thing again and this time the shiver went right down to her toes. To break the mood she said the first thing that came into her head. 'Are you saying I'm so heavy I bogged my chair?'

His teeth flashed as he glanced at her figure. 'No.'

He nodded at the waiter to say they'd be back and they took the few steps to the water's edge and began walking along towards the airport in the distance. They didn't speak but strangely it wasn't as awkward as she'd thought it would be.

The waves lapped politely, no big chasers in the occasional wash up like happened at home, just gentle lapping that never threatened her light slides, or her concentration at maintaining a safe distance.

The sand crunched firmly beneath their feet and the stars overhead twinkled benignly down on them. She could feel her annoyance from his refusal to discuss his life recede like the water beside her and she let it go.

It didn't matter. Really it didn't. She didn't know him. Probably wouldn't see him again and it had been a very pleasant meal.

Then he ruined it. 'Any chance of meeting up tomorrow?'

She fought back the overreaction she wanted to make, like a full-throated scream of *Yes*, and impressed herself by the way her answer slid out quite lightly. 'No.'

'The day after?'

She wanted a flirtation, not an affair. Already she was too aware of every facial expression, every shrug of those lovely shoulders and the strength in those powerful legs that walked beside her. Sensory overload. She glanced at him. 'Thanks for dinner. Can we go back now?'

Harry felt her pull away, even though her body didn't move. It was a subtle stiffening and leaning to increase the distance between them. Unmistakable. Well, he'd blown that. Not something he was used to doing but he was just out of practice. Funny how he could be smooth with someone he didn't care how it went with and a bumbling idiot with someone he wanted to impress.

Now, why was he trying to impress her? He slanted a glance at Bonnie of the determined chin and wondered why as they walked back to their table. He liked it that she was taller than most women, though she was a little frail. He could easily imagine being able to span her waist with his hands, and maybe he should insist on dessert to fatten her up.

She seemed too fragile to him. Maybe nursing her gran had really taken it out of her. He could feel the swell of empathy pulling bricks out of the walls he'd built over the last two years, snapping mortar and the solid pattern of layers like a berserk tradesman. Now, how had he left himself open to that?

His sensible side began a mental slurry of cement on the cracks and crumbles and hardened his heart. Then the words came easily.

'I'll pay the bill and take you home, then.'

CHAPTER THREE

IN THE early hours of the morning Harry lay on his side and gazed out over the beach. He watched the stars inch their way across the sky. He'd tried turning his back on them but he knew they were there. Laughing at him. He couldn't remember the last time he'd tossed and turned over a woman. Well, he could but he didn't want to remember that disaster.

But Bonnie was different, softer, like a calm place to sit and enjoy situations and surroundings he'd forgotten how to enjoy. And that tinge of sadness around her sat like a mist he wanted to wave away. Problem was that voice in his head had burnt him before. He squeezed his pillow again and buried his ear into the packed softness of feathers. Softness was a pain.

* * *

Next morning, he found himself standing beside her breakfast table. Just in case she'd changed her mind. 'Good morning, Bonnie.'

Bonnie shook her head. Obviously Harry didn't understand no. Which for an intelligent man seemed a little bizarre.

She took a careful sip of her tea, savoured the honey—Bali had lovely black tea—and ignored the little glow that wasn't leaf-related. 'Good morning, Harry.'

'You must be Bonnie's friends.' He glanced at the girls as if to check their response to her fake name. Bonnie's smile kicked. Now, that was gold.

'May I join you?' His open-necked shirt exposed a strong brown throat and the buttons strained as he leaned over the table. Her poor young friends nearly swallowed their spoons. Too much testosterone this early in the morning.

Sacha stuttered. 'O-of course.' With cheeks like fairy floss she practically offered him her own chair, then turned wondering eyes on Bonnie. 'You said it was a one-off.'

It was a six-seater table. Bonnie made a note to herself to insist on a table that would only seat three next time. 'He's obviously slow on the uptake.'

Sacha waved him into a bamboo chair and he sat down. 'I wondered if I could interest you ladies in a bike ride down Mt Agung. I have a friend who runs tours and he's got a couple of places left this morning.'

'Two or three?' Bonnie asked sweetly. It was dare for him to be specific. He smiled sweetly at her.

'Three or four.'

'Even room for you?' Bonnie sighed. Before he could answer, Jacinta dropped her shoulders and Sacha did too. 'We're out. We booked that cooking class thing today.'

Harry attempted to look disappointed. 'And you?'

'It really is Bonnie, you know.' She smiled sweetly. Did she want to spend a whole day with this guy? Or would she spend it by herself, wishing she'd gone with him?

After the call last night this was her last full day and the bike ride sounded ideal. She'd see the countryside after all and she needed to break out of this cloud of apathy she'd been in for the last few months. He was certainly helping there.

It seemed unlikely he'd attempt to race her off in a pack of cyclists. And she had some say in it. 'What time is this ride and how do I know it really exists?'

'You do have a nastily suspicious mind.' He produced a brochure and a mobile phone. 'But I expected that. You could ring Wayan and ask him.'

She took the glossy pamphlet and turned it over in her hands. The number stood out plainly and she was very tempted to do it. He was daring her now and she couldn't decide if he was real or fake. He'd be great at poker.

He looked suspiciously ready to go in that open-necked shirt that dared her to peek at the strong column of his throat but she wasn't going to.

He wore different blue jeans and scuffed joggers that might have been expensive in their heyday, and that watch, which she'd decided was definitely not real. Like him.

There, she'd made a decision. If the watch was fake, he was fake. She'd buy one in the women's version and this man would know the right vendor on the street. 'Where'd you buy your watch?'

'Geneva.'

She wrinkled her nose. There was no deception in the answer. She'd been wrong. Again. 'What time is pick-up?'

'Half an hour.' He was rushing her. He liked to do that but she'd lost the bet with herself so she had to go. For an internal argument it was pretty thin. It was just so darned hard to say no to someone who made her smile. At least on the inside.

The bus had seen better days but the grins of the tour guides were shiny new. Typically Balinese, they oozed warmth and fun and plea-sure at the company of tourists and the chance to show off their culture and country. Something a lot of countries could learn from, Bonnie mused as she was helped into the bus.

Four couples made up the bus passengers when they started again—two young female school-teachers from Portugal, two chefs from France, a fitness instructor and his wife from the States, and Harry and Bonnie from Australia.

Bonnie was jammed against the window, which in itself was a good thing and not only for the view. It was a bit like choosing a window seat on the plane. You could create your own space if you needed. But she could still feel the warmth from Harry's jeans-clad leg against hers and that wasn't going away unless she broke the safety glass.

Harry laughed and joked with the others around them about accents and travel mishaps, a different person from the man she'd seen yesterday at the pool. Aloof and cynical seemed to have stayed home today. So why'd he been so threatened yesterday? Interesting.

Bonnie found herself relaxing back with a little proprietorial smile that said she was here—with him—as the little bus ground up the mountain. Until she realised her sin and it slipped from her face.

Then she frowned. Crazy. This was holiday, short-term, transient. Even more transient than she'd anticipated. Enjoy the moment, enjoy the company and most of all enjoy Harry. She was on vacation, for goodness' sake, and she'd soon be at the new job, wishing she had. This was safe.

Harry saw the moment Bonnie became a part of the group and suddenly the day seemed brighter. She smiled at him and for that moment the sadness he'd glimpsed in her eyes was gone. He felt his breath kick somewhere at the back of his throat and his chest expanded. He'd done that. He'd helped her feel better. And it felt good.

That was when he reminded himself to be careful.

He looked away from her profile, past the itching temptation to study the bones of her face and out the window towards the ancient volcano as it came into sight. Terraced rice fields skirted the mountains like layers on a brilliant green wedding cake and that thought made him shudder.

This wasn't him. Connecting with women was so not on his programme. He'd been there and the pain was so great he wasn't climbing that volcano so he could fall off again. He'd pulled himself away from all he knew, bolted home to Bali, the one place where he could drift and nobody would think it out of the ordinary. A place he could drown out the voice in his head that said he didn't want this empty life but he wasn't willing to risk more pain.

'Is that a volcano?' Bonnie turned towards him and her eyes were like the rice fields outside the window—iridescent with life.

He ran his hand down his face to clear any dumb expression he might've been left with. 'Yes, Mt Agung. We'll be having morning tea at the restaurant above Mt Batur, at Kintamani—lots of old lava at the base of that one. Then we'll pick up the bikes at a village and ride downhill until we get to the river.' He shut his mouth. He was rambling.

'So how many times have you done this?'

He shrugged. 'A few.' Too many. 'Sometimes I help out when they're short of supervising riders, and it's always a great day.' Brainless, time consuming, just what he wanted.

She tilted her head. 'You said you were visiting. How long have you been here this time?'

'On and off, nine months this time.' She was studying him and he could feel his face freeze with the old barriers at giving anything away.

'A whole pregnancy,' she said, and he winced. Great timing. A good boot to the guts like he needed to stop the rot. Ironic.

He turned away and spoke to the Portuguese girl about surfing, blocking Bonnie out, and yet still he felt it when she withdrew her attention and looked back out the window. His breath eased out. The Portuguese girl batted her eyelashes at him but her interest didn't faze him like Bonnie's did. Funny, that.

Finally they made it to the first stop. He'd never noticed the trip taking so long before and he felt like shaking himself like a dog to get out of Bonnie's aura. He'd been mad to ask her out today. Not just mad. Dangerously insane.

For Bonnie, the view from the restaurant overlooking the volcano at Kintamani took her breath, and thankfully her mind, off the puzzle of the man next to her.

From where she stood overlooking the valley, because the restaurant walkway hung over the cliff, the view presented the huge lake and black scarring of the lava across the valley floor. Great gaping inverted cones up the side of Mt Batur showed the force of the volcanic activity.

'When was the last eruption?' She asked the question without looking at him. She didn't have to turn to know he was right there. Her sensory receptors had warned her.

'Nineteen ninety-four. One of the earlier ones

swallowed the temple at Kintamani village. The western slopes are closed at the moment. The seismological institute thinks there's risk of further eruptions. Pity. It's a great walk to the rim for sunrise.'

Bonnie looked through the window into the restaurant at the rice and crêpes waiting, very strange morning tea on offer, and glanced at the view again. 'What's the lava like up close?

'Hard and black. I rode across the whole field on a motorbike years ago and it was like jagged corrugated iron. The locals use it for building and you can see the areas where the lava's been quarried.'

As a guide he was knowledgeable, though distracting from the view, enthusiastic about local history, just not good at being consistently relaxing, and she couldn't see much of the yoga student this morning.

Then again, maybe it wasn't his fault because half an hour later, when she followed the others back to the bus and climbed in, it was Harry's leg alongside hers that she was waiting for. In fact, she could feel little waves of anticipation building as she sat down.

Disappointingly, this time they didn't touch. Interesting and a little unacceptable, and she wasn't quite sure how he managed it. As an experiment she allowed her knee to accidentally knock against his while she looked out the window and there was no doubt he shifted further away.

Definite reversal of the forces of attraction. She'd blotted her copybook somehow. Maybe it was the crack about pregnancy.

On her recent history of foot-in-mouth moments he'd probably lost a car full of children too. She sighed and then shrugged. This was why she didn't get involved with men. Too complicated and distracting. It was a beautiful day and she was going to enjoy it if it killed her. She smiled to herself. Or him.

Wayan, their guide, had spent the last five minutes of travel explaining about luwak coffee and the main export for the plantation they were about to visit, but Bonnie had faded out.

So when the bus trundled into a dusty car park alongside other decrepit buses all shaded by over-hanging trees and vines, she wondered if this was where the bike ride started.

She was thinking about the last man she'd fallen for and how that whole fiasco had poisoned her life. How, foolishly, she'd thought they'd planned the whole wedding thing, the first two years of saving, agreed on children, she'd put her savings with his for the deposit on their dream home.

She'd come home shattered from nursing her gran, vaguely aware she hadn't paid much atten-tion to him for the last hard few weeks, and when she had come back for the comfort he'd prom-ised—he'd been gone, along with her money. Not that she'd cared about that at that point.

'And it's the most expensive coffee in the world.'

Well, she couldn't afford that. Bonnie zoned in again and followed Wayan through the over-hanging forest, listening as he identified coffee in various stages, tree types and fruit, aware of Harry at her shoulder not saying anything.

Finally they came to the cage where the luwak slept, incarcerated. Bonnie looked at Harry and whispered, 'What the heck is a luwak?' Harry gestured to Wayan and smiled and she tried to catch up.

'We leave them for one day in the cage,' Wayan told them, 'and then set them free again. It is only so you can see the actual animal. Asian palm civets—also known as luwaks here—normally sleep and hide at the time people visit the plantation.'

They all stared into the dark cage and tried to see the small furry animal, which looked a little like a cat-faced possum or smaller mongoose.

She whispered to Harry, 'I don't get it. How does it make coffee?'

He tilted his head and studied her genuine bafflement. A slow smile curved his lips. 'You weren't listening.'

'I might have missed a bit.' She shrugged.

Harry tilted his head and she could feel his scrutiny. Could feel the heat in her cheeks at his amusement. He was laughing at her—not with her—and she didn't like it.

'He's been talking about it for the last ten minutes.'

'So?' She held out her hands, frustrated by his teasing. 'Tell me now.'

Harry grinned. 'Luwaks are an alternative to conventional coffee processing. They process the beans internally.' He grinned again as she shrugged and shook her head, obviously not getting it. 'You don't pick the beans off the trees— you follow the luwaks around with a shovel.'

'They poo it?' Bonnie blinked. 'You're kidding me?'

Harry laughed out loud and suddenly the rapport between them was back in full force. 'I kid you not.'

He patted her shoulder. 'You get to try some soon. Luwaks only choose to eat the very best coffee beans, and they have a great internal processing unit that still leaves the coffee bean whole when they're…' he paused and grinned again '…finished with it.'

Bonnie shook her head. 'No way.' When had they discussed this? Had Wayan said that in the bus? How would this be the most expensive coffee in the world?

'They wash the beans,' Harry said blandly, but she could see the unholy amusement in his eyes. Just looking at him made her smile and boosted her fragile self-esteem that Jeremy had injured so badly. That was the point when she should have run away.

Bonnie screwed up her face and Harry laughed out loud. 'Double dare you.'

Drink second-hand coffee beans? 'I don't think so.'

'In the States it sells for more than a hundred bucks a pound. Not something you'll have a lot of chance to try again.'

True. But who'd want to? She followed Harry

through to the coffee tables, where the rest of the group were ordering their coffee, and before she knew it she was sitting beside Harry with a steaming cup of black brew in front of her.

And everyone else seemed to be tasting it. *Ew.*

She looked around again and the Portuguese girls were chatting up the chefs as they sipped, and everyone still looked happy with their experience.

She was the only one not drinking. Even Harry had his cup.

Bonnie took a cautious sip. 'It tastes a bit like mocha.'

Harry raised his eyebrows. 'Is that what that is?'

He could tease. She put her cup down. 'Well, at least I tried it.'

Harry gave up his short-lived attempt to keep his distance with her. She delighted him with her honesty. She couldn't hide a single thought with those straightforward eyes of hers. Talk about windows to the soul. They telegraphed every thought and emotion like a green neon sign. Scary, and despite her antsy, prickly little exterior he could feel the need to protect her from the world like a growing seed inside him.

Hopefully that little weed of concern for her would die from lack of sunlight when she flew away. But for the moment he could give in to these crazy feelings because she'd only be there for a few days and he had no plans.

He could feel the chuckle in his chest as she manfully swallowed the coffee she didn't want. He reached across the table and scooped her hand into his, and she let her fingers lie there. It felt good to have her warm and protected by him. He tried not to see the grin of Wayan, who'd never seen Harry so circumspect with a young woman in all the time he'd known him.

Bonnie couldn't remember the last time she'd held hands with a man. Her fiancé hadn't been into hand-holding and it had almost been worth a taste of kopi luwak coffee for the buzz of feeling a situation she hadn't tried before.

Like she belonged with Harry for this minute anyway. She was having a holiday fling, almost. Good grief. Her girlfriends in Darwin would be whooping with joy.

'Come on, the bus is leaving, you can leave the last bit. We get to find our bikes now and the real fun begins.' They held hands all the way to the bus and it felt 'nice'.

Back on the bus, this time his hip returned to rest against hers again and their knees bumped companionably together as the bus ground down the hill. It was as good as she'd remembered and she smiled secretly at her own reflection in the window.

The village that housed the bikes seemed deserted but Harry chose for her the least battered pushbike, no doubt drawing on his experience of bike fallibility, and the tread on the narrow tyres at least looked new.

'Have a little pedal around here while everyone gets their bike,' he said, and she climbed on with a nervous grimace. It had been years and she fought the tremble in her knees as she took off.

At least she could touch the ground easily. The Portuguese girl had a death wobble until Harry stopped her and put her seat down for safety. Bonnie liked it that he cared.

Between Harry and the Balinese guides, everyone had their bikes set to go within ten minutes, bottles of water were handed out and then the lead rider took off with all his less confident ducklings behind him. Everyone except Harry and the fitness instructor rode stiffly. Bonnie and Harry brought up the rear, which seemed to set them apart in their own world.

The descent started out gradual. A bit like the way she'd little by little become relaxed around Harry, though he'd become slightly anxious when she'd nearly steered her bike into an unexpected drain at the side of the road.

'That ditch would have swallowed you. Stay nearer the centre,' Harry pleaded as she veered his way again suddenly to avert another catastrophe.

From then on he positioned his bike to keep her out of the gutter.

'Whew.' She took her hand off the handle to dry her sweaty palms on her used-to-be-white trousers. 'How embarrassing it would be to wipe out in the first kilometre.'

'Or worse,' he muttered, and glanced across at her. 'You can't just choose an orthopaedic surgeon here, you know.'

Bonnie laughed. 'I missed the hole. Nothing to worry about.' In fact, she felt remarkably relaxed now that the initial wobbles had disappeared.

The sun was shining, the road had the occasional country vehicle, but most of the time it was just the bike riders, fields and villages as they sailed past.

Harry pointed out features of different village temples, family buildings and the census plaques on top of the entry arches, which Bonnie had never noticed before.

'So each census tag has how many sons and their families, and how many adults and children live in the family compound.'

Bonnie slowed as they peddled past the entrance to another family compound and this time she could make out the little strokes denoting the family members. 'Cool. So there's five children in that compound.'

'Yep.' He looked quite pleased she was interested but it was no hardship. She found the insight into Balinese culture fascinating. And it was also attractive that Harry wanted to share his own interest with her.

Too many things were attractive about him. 'You care about these people, don't you? You're not just interested in them out of curiosity.'

He nodded. 'Of course. I've spent a lot of time here and anyone who does that comes to appreciate Bali and her people.'

'So why don't you work here?'

'I do a bit.' He didn't enlarge on it. Instead he said, 'My friend was born in a village near here.

Sometimes the kids run out to wave as we ride by. They'll hold their hands out for a high five. It can give you a fright.'

The rest of the bike riders had stopped up ahead. There was a generalised wobble as they all put their feet down and Bonnie was no exception. She glanced at Harry's face as he tried to hide his grin. 'Don't even think about laughing.'

She pretended to frown at him and he held up his hands as if to say, 'Never.'

'We'll go through the village here, and then later on you'll be able to recognise the layout and functions of the buildings and compounds we still have to go past.'

She glanced down the discreet dirt track between the buildings and couldn't help feeling a little uncomfortable at the invasion of privacy. There seemed to be people at work in each section but none of them appeared fazed by the intrusion.

The whole compound looked sparse and basic. Not a place that was used to luxuries she took for granted every day. Happy children ran up and down with shrieks of merriment and a young father smiled at them as he plaited strips of thin bamboo with his tiny son.

Bonnie lowered her voice and leant closer to Harry. 'So what do they do for wages here?'

'Bamboo production.' He pointed to the huge stand of thick bamboo that grew at the bottom of the street. 'Dewi, here, is a skilled plaiter and his sheets of bamboo matting are used for the internal ceilings of most types of buildings. When you go back to your hotel you'll notice that the roof in your bedroom is made up of this plaited bamboo. It'll be from a village like this. Dewi's work is much sought after.'

Bonnie smiled at the young Balinese man and she couldn't help her wider grin when she realised his son was trying to plait a smaller version of his father's work. His little face was screwed up in concentration as he laboriously weaved.

The father spoke in Balinese and Harry laughed and answered him, then turned to Bonnie. 'He said his son looks perfect now but he'll get sick of it soon and start to cause mischief.'

'Where's his mother?'

Harry pointed to a covered work area ahead. 'She's stripping the bamboo with his grand-mother, further down. Each villager does part of the process, from the man beside the bamboo who harvests to those that split it in half then quarters and pass it on to the next section, who keep thinning it down until Dewi has workable strips to weave with.'

They moved past the sections, the tourists snap-ping pictures and watching the villagers work, and all the time Harry spoke to the villagers in their own language, smiling and greeting them by name.

It was interesting to Bonnie how the people they met hailed Harry, patted him on the back, called out to him, considering he seemed tran-sient, and she wondered if he ever thought of when he would leave and get on with his life.

But why should she care? She could feel a

creeping sense of evangelistic purpose to save Harry's working soul and she stamped it down.

Stop it. He'd not thank her for it and it was none of her business. He was just a man she'd met. But a place inside her ached for the occasional glimpse of the caring, lost soul he tried to hide. She pulled her thoughts away and concentrated on village life.

She admired the one cow the family owned, the eldest son's pride and joy and, according to Harry, a huge investment. The cow chewed placidly and stared at them from a private sheltered bale, a long-lashed, happy cow, living in Utopia.

Pigs snorted in muddy pens and chickens darted underfoot, chased by a red-combed rooster, and Harry told her the wives cared for the other animals while the husbands cared for the cow.

Consistently, it seemed Harry picked up on her interest when the guide spoke of traditions and when he mentioned the ceremonies each family was responsible for.

Harry enlarged on the subject after Wayan had

moved on. 'The cost of a burial sometimes take years for a family to save for—it can cost the same as their one cow. But the family are happy to ensure their relation is cremated with a full and proper celebration.

She looked around at the bare compound. 'What if the family can't afford a funeral when someone dies?'

'The person is temporarily buried, maybe a year or two, and exhumed when they can afford it. Or sometimes when another family is having a funeral they share the costs with several families who have members to bury. But it's a necessary expenditure for ancestor status.'

Harry waved at another man and as he stopped to talk Bonnie caught the eye of a young pregnant woman sitting quietly in the doorway of a building, slicing ginger.

There was something about the way she held her neck stiffly that attracted Bonnie's attention and she drifted over to say hello.

The young woman peeled the grey root swiftly

and surely but every few minutes her face changed and she glanced down at her stomach. When she looked up she must have seen the concern in Bonnie's eyes because she shook her head as if to say it was nothing.

Bonnie allowed her own glance to drift down and tried to estimate the gestation of the pregnancy. Nearly full term, that was for sure, but not a big baby. Harry wandered off to talk to the Portuguese couple and Bonnie edged towards the doorway.

'Hello. I'm Bonnie. I'm afraid I don't speak much Balinese.'

'I am Mardi.' The young woman's voice was very soft and to Bonnie's relief quietly confident with her English. 'I worked in a restaurant before I married my husband and speak good English.'

'You're very clever. My Indonesian is bad apart from *hello* and *good morning*.' She smiled. 'Is your baby giving you pains?'

Mardi glanced down at her stomach with a

gentle smile. 'A little. But he is not due until next month. It has happened for a little while each day this last week so I'm hoping my belly will go soon to sleep.'

CHAPTER FOUR

JUDGING from the changing expressions on the young woman's face, Bonnie doubted these pains would go away.

Bonnie waited for the strain to ease from Mardi's face again. Pretty decent contraction, she thought. When it had gone she said, 'Maybe she or he has decided to come today.'

Mardi looked down at the brown dust beneath her feet. 'Not today. My husband is away working to save money. We cannot afford the midwife yet.'

Bonnie wasn't sure how that worked when nature didn't play the game. 'What about the hospital?'

Calmly Mardi shook her head and her thick black hair barely moved in the coiled bun. 'The hospital costs are even greater.' She grimaced again and Bonnie frowned.

'Looks like labour to me,' Bonnie muttered under her breath. She'd seen quite a few. 'Have the pains been this close and strong before?'

Mardi shook her head and this time Bonnie saw the start of the glint of tears in her beautiful brown eyes. 'Perhaps I am a little fearful.'

Fear was the last thing a woman in labour needed. 'Is your husband's mother here?'

Mardi's coil shifted slightly again. 'She died at his birth. Which is why he wishes for me to have the midwife. His grandmother is here, but she cannot see well. His brother's wife is here and had one son in the hospital.'

Bonnie wanted to hug her but she also didn't want to intrude if she wasn't wanted. 'I'm a mid-wife in Australia. Can I help you?'

Bonnie glanced over her shoulder, hoping to catch the eye of Harry, but he was still laughing with the Portuguese girls.

She glared at him in frustration. As if she'd

touched him, or thrown something at him, he stopped what he was saying and glanced her way. Without a word he crossed the road to her side.

He nodded at Mardi and lowered his voice as he looked at Bonnie. 'Is everything all right?'

Bonnie was thrown for a moment. Coincidence? Telepathy? She had no idea how that had worked. He'd been receptive and come quickly. The concept that she'd called him without words sent a trickle of unease through her. That was too much connection.

No. Just coincidence, that's all.

The thought was closely followed by the priorities she'd let slip as Mardi drew another sharp breath. 'We need to find Mardi's husband because she's going into labour.'

Bonnie had no doubt now. Just looking at Mardi, anyone would tell the time for false labour had passed and she'd bet her borrowed pushbike the baby would come today. 'He's away to save money for the midwife.'

To her surprise Harry paled and then seemed

to shake himself into sense. His eyes narrowed and she could almost see his mind weighing the options. For a carefree surfer he was on the ball quickly. 'I'll take you to the hospital. The backup vehicle for the bike ride is parked outside.'

One lone tear slid down Mardi's cheek. 'I don't want to go to the hospital without my husband. I will wait for him.'

'Hospitals cost a lot,' Bonnie murmured quietly, as if mentioning a common fact, and Harry looked at her and nodded but he wasn't happy.

He rubbed his neck. 'But will that baby wait for you both?' Harry said what Bonnie was thinking. Mardi bit back a moan and Harry looked at Bonnie.

A glance akin to horror lurked in his eyes, again totally unexpected. But she guessed laypeople were often fazed by the myths and misconceptions surrounding childbirth.

'Birth's a normal event,' she couldn't help saying. 'Could you get Mardi's sister-in-law, please? And a doctor, if you can find one.' Bonnie rested her hand on Mardi's arm. 'Perhaps we could go to your house and you could collect what you would need to take with you, for when your husband arrives?'

In fact, Bonnie wanted to see where they could have this baby if it came more quickly than any of them anticipated.

'We could do that,' Mardi whispered, and she stood gingerly when the next contraction had passed. Bonnie mentally rifled through the belongings she had on her that could be helpful, but she'd only carried a waist pack that held very little.

She gave herself a mental shake. Harry would sort something out if she asked him. The important thing was to get Mardi comfortable and semiprepared for her baby's possibly precipitous arrival.

This wasn't an unusual scenario in Outback Australia if a baby arrived early and one that didn't faze Bonnie too much. Though it would've been nice if there was a doctor around to share the load, in case of an emergency. She doubted she'd be legal to practise in a foreign country.

Harry strode off to search out Mardi's sister-in-law and as he walked he fumed at the cruelty of fate.

Why now, why here, why him? It was all very well for Bonnie to be blasé about birth, typical midwife, but she hadn't seen what he had. The last thing he wanted was a medical catastrophe in a Third World village. He'd have to be the doctor, get involved, and probably still not be able to improve the outcome.

He should never have come here with her. It was his own stupid fault. He'd known women were trouble he needed to avoid.

He caught sight of his quarry, Mardi's sister-in-law, and hastened his footsteps. Maybe if they found Mardi's husband quickly they could still get to the hospital in time. But if he'd interpreted Bonnie's face correctly, she had her doubts. He had his own.

Bonnie and Mardi had left the industrious

centre of the village and moved into the narrow street of the family dwellings. Bonnie counted four buildings in a smaller compound and one stood higher than the rest, with steep steps leading up to the small veranda.

Mardi intercepted Bonnie's glance. 'My husband's grandparents' house. The grandparent house is higher than others as a mark of respect. As it should be.'

Mardi gestured down at a round shiny river rock to the left of the grandparent's steep steps. 'There lies the placenta of my husband's nephew. It is my husband's task to clean and bury our child's placenta below these steps.'

'So one stone, one grandchild?'

'That is correct. And should I have a girl it would be buried on the right side of the step.'

Bonnie grinned. She loved it. This was delicious food for a midwife's soul. Fabulous information, and she wondered if Harry was aware of it.

The next building they passed contained two

sparse kitchens, side by side, and Mardi glanced inside. Despite her worries, Mardi smiled. 'This kitchen is mine, and the other belongs to my husband's brother's wife, Nyomen. It is said peace cannot exist if two women have to share a kitchen.'

'What a sensible arrangement.' Bonnie smiled with her. 'I can see that everyone lives very close together here.'

'Family is very important in Bali.' They both slipped off their shoes and Mardi gestured to Bonnie to precede her up the stairs to a room that shared a veranda with another room. 'This is my home. Everybody knows everyone else's business. We share all joys and sorrows. You cannot help but do so when we live this close.'

'And what is the other building that looks like a covered platform?'

'That is where we hold our ceremonies. Where my child will be blessed when three months old and can first touch the ground.'

Bonnie couldn't help a brief sidetrack. 'Three months before a baby can touch the ground?'

Mardi nodded. 'To touch the ground before then would allow the chance of evil spirits to enter a child.'

She'd bet some parents at home would disagree with that but she could see the warmth and benefit in a child knowing a pair of arms would always be there for them. No wonder the Balinese people smiled so much—they knew how much love and care was taken of them from the moment of birth.

Mardi stopped and leant against the doorframe. Bonnie waited quietly beside her and let her thoughts drift into that distant space she seemed to go to when she was waiting with a woman— not really a daydream when she thought of other things, more of a holding pattern that didn't use any energy or was distracting for the woman, that just 'was', while she waited.

The pain eased and Mardi moved inside the

house just as her sister-in-law, Nyomen, arrived with Harry and glided up the stairs to help.

The two women embraced and Bonnie moved back to the edge of the veranda as Nyomen gathered several sarongs and a water bottle.

When the young mother-to-be stopped and leant against her sister-in-law again, Bonnie leant down to speak to Harry. 'Is her husband coming?'

Harry nodded stiffly, strain in every line of his body. 'He should be here soon.'

Good. But she doubted this baby would wait. 'So, ever been present for a birth, Harry?' His face closed and she could feel her own forehead crease. That looked bad.

So when he said, 'No,' she was almost surprised.

'Ah.' Pretending not to be surprised. 'That explains your nerves. Everything will be fine.'

'No, thanks. Let's get her out of here.' Harry's face held the granite stiffness she'd seen at the pool the day she'd first seen him. There were things going on here she couldn't fully fathom and unfortunately now wasn't the time to ask.

She rested her hand on his arm and he looked at her. 'We'll all be fine.' Bonnie actually felt sorry for him. 'She won't go to the hospital until her husband arrives. I'm afraid it's too late for that, anyway.'

She thought he'd heard her and accepted that, but then he shook his head as if waking from a trance. 'It's not too late. I'm not stupid. Let's grab her and go.'

She touched his arm again. 'Harry. Listen to me.' Her voice was very quiet so as not to disturb the labouring woman. 'And what? Have the baby in that old bus?'

She saw the moment when he really saw her, saw her logic, had to accept reality and the impending birth. He ran his hands through his hair and gradually his face softened, though there was no doubting his reluctance to face the inevitable. She saw the flash of pain that followed and was quickly hidden. 'You're right. I'm sorry. Lost it for a moment there.'

'It must have been a very bad experience,' she said quietly. There was more history here than she'd anticipated. 'What can I do to help you, Harry?'

'Nothing.' He glanced at her and then away. Every barrier in place shielding him from her empathy. 'Now, what do you need?'

He was right. Maybe she had it wrong. This was the response she'd expected from Harry. Thank goodness. She felt the pack around her waist and undid the zipper.

'I don't imagine I'll be doing much. I just want to be here to help keep Mardi and her baby safe. Maybe good old-fashioned boiling water to sterilise some string and a knife to cut the cord.' She patted the miniature bottle of hand-sanitiser she always kept in her bag. 'Or I could clean the knife with this.' She looked around. 'And maybe a dish of warm water to sponge Mardi with afterwards.'

'What about the drugs you won't have?'

It seemed a strange thing to say but she shrugged it off. 'She's healthy and we don't have any. She'll breastfeed. This is what women are designed to do. Her body will look after her. Why should she be unlucky?'

He held up his hands. 'Okay. Just thought I'd mention it.'

'Maybe there is one thing. Will you reassure Mardi and Nyomen I'm a midwife and I'd like to stay until after the baby is born if her husband doesn't arrive in time? The most important thing is for her not to be frightened.'

He sighed. 'I can do that.' And more quietly so she only just heard, 'That's about all I'm good for.'

When he'd finished speaking the two women nodded their consent, and there was relief in both faces, relief that made Harry grimace as he turned back to her.

'I'll go see about the string and the water.'

Mardi made a small moaning noise, and Nyomen gestured to Bonnie to come inside the house. The women had made a small bed on the floor, and a neat pile of older sarongs had been placed beside her.

Bonnie washed her hands with the antiseptic, and offered it to the other women. Then she sat back a little and folded her hands. There was nothing she could do. She could see the baby moving under his mother's loosened sarong so that was a good sign. It was time to wait.

By the time Harry returned they'd set up a little screen with another sarong and the elderly grandmother was also in the room.

He wished himself anywhere but there. Even back out on the street. Back with the tourists. His nerves crawled with anxiety—not a normal reaction for a damn doctor, he told himself, but this was how things went wrong. This was what he'd decided he'd never get involved in again. Had told himself he didn't have to get involved with again because he could easily avoid becoming drawn in.

How Bonnie had stopped him from picking up

Mardi and rushing her to the hospital he didn't know. But then, if she was as close as Bonnie said, the idea of the baby being born halfway down the mountain was no better anyway.

The sudden unmistakable sound of a baby's wail drifted from the room above him, and he looked up to hear the muted voices of happy women and even a laugh from the grandmother. His shoulders sagged and he felt like dropping his head into his hands as well.

Relief flooded over him. Waves of emotion he hadn't wanted. Overwhelming, and it was harrowing how close he'd been to inappropriate action. Maybe it was time to rationalise how much he needed to confront his issues.

He almost wished he hadn't met this pesky midwife, but couldn't quite convince himself that was true.

The relief inside expanded into unexpected pride—for clever Mardi, the unfazeable Bonnie, and the fact that he had trusted enough. Just.

The sound of running feet heralded the arrival

of Mardi's stunned husband, and the poor man kicked his shoes off and bolted up the stairs to greet his wife and new daughter. Harry smiled at the voluble thanks that were being heaped on Bonnie's head. He let the sounds wash over him. He'd translate when they were on their own.

Finally Bonnie reappeared, a huge smile on her face, her eyes alight with the joy of the moment, and he could see how she revelled in her vocation. Lucky her. But he couldn't help that darker sliver of reality that said she'd been lucky.

Some people weren't that lucky.

Bonnie drifted out of the compound on a high, stunned again at the beauty and simplicity of childbirth, the pure blessing of a newborn baby and the luck of being a witness to it all.

Then she realised the bike ride had gone on without them.

'We'll catch them at lunch.' Harry smiled at her, but the strain hadn't been erased from his features and he looked far from carefree and relaxed. 'I thought it might be therapeutic to just keep rolling down the hill to soak in the morning rather than get a lift to catch up with the others.'

'Perfect.' He was right. She still had that smile on her face from the birth and everything seemed brighter and more precious as they cycled along.

'I gather there were no hitches to the birth?'

She heard him but it took her a couple of seconds to pull her brain back from euphoria. 'Baby's shoulders were a little tight but a change in position sorted that.' Joy bubbled and sang inside her and she wouldn't have given away this day for the world.

She watched Harry bounce airborne over a little hump in the road and she laughed out loud.

The birth had been incredible, Mardi a delight and the baby so gorgeous and big-eyed it brought the tears to her face again just remembering.

Harry felt like a heel. And a surly one at that. He wanted to share her joy but his mind kept returning to what could have gone wrong. To what had gone wrong in the past. He was so used to shutting people down he'd got out of practice at opening up. And there was something about Bonnie that made him want to share a little of himself for the first time in a long time.

She'd been so incredible at the village and he shuddered to think he might have been on his own and would have had to cope with that.

Though she was smiling when he looked back, he caught a glint of tears in her eyes and the sight nearly knocked him off his bike. He'd upset her. Harry veered closer. 'Are you all right?'

'Yes.' The smile she turned on him was even more of an assault than her tears. 'Just reliving the moment.'

The birth was making her emotional, not him. He'd forgotten how different women's thought processes were from men's.

The last thing he wanted to do was relive his trepidation during the birth. 'No, thanks,' Harry muttered, and she smiled again as if she understood. But how could she? She had no idea.

'Thanks for being there, Harry.'

He could feel those damn walls crumbling all over. 'Don't ask again.'

'Now who's the wimp?' she teased him. Something had changed for ever between them. They could never really be strangers again after this and they both knew it.

Was he a wimp? No doubt of that. He didn't say anything and she smiled again.

'This is so great. Thanks for finishing the ride. It would have been such an anticlimax to climb back into the bus and get dropped back at the hotel.'

'Hmm.' But then he looked across at her and couldn't help agreeing with her. The words came out before he realised what he'd been going to say. 'You're pretty amazing, you know.'

She shook her head and her ponytail wagged. 'Not me. It's birthing women who're amazing.'

'Spare me from the midwife.' He rolled his eyes.

Her face shifted to serious, the softness of laughter fading away, and he had the feeling she was going to say something he wouldn't like. 'Yes, I will. Spare you my presence. Tomorrow morning, when I fly back to Australia.'

'Tomorrow?' That hit him harder than he would have believed possible. 'I thought you had another couple of days?'

She shrugged her shoulders and the bike wobbled. He wished she wouldn't do that. 'I had a call last night, and they're short at my next posting.' She glanced at him. 'The fill-in medical officer isn't going to show and I'm flying back tomorrow to help cover.'

Too soon. Far too soon. But how ironic. She was going to Uluru early and it was his fault. 'It's not your problem until you start.'

She flicked a frown at him before looking back at the road.

She was going. Just when he'd dared to risk opening up. *See*, he told himself. *You are better pushing people away.*

Then she said, 'Have you always been like this?'

'Like what?'

'Egotistical, self-absorbed.' The words hit him like the splashes of mud he'd just pedalled through. Sticking to him. Was he? Or just plain scared?

They were passing through a village and two young boys ran out holding up their hands. Bonnie swerved because she wasn't concentrating and nearly collided with Harry, who took evasive action more easily than she had.

'Whoa, there,' Harry cautioned, though he still managed to high-five the two boys. Squeals of delight followed them down the road and he could feel a smile tug at his lips. He did enjoy seeing the village children.

She looked ahead to rice paddies and sighed. 'It must be hard work in there.' Just like that. She'd brushed him off. He'd asked her to but now he wasn't sure he liked the feeling she could do it so easily. It was darned good she was leaving tomorrow.

'Follow me,' Harry steered them onto a smaller track. 'This one comes out between the fields.'

They bumped down a rocky incline and suddenly the way was smooth again as they hit a concrete path that rose between the fields and separated one rice paddy from the next. Their bikes were at waist-level with the workers and several called out to Harry as they pedalled past.

Bonnie would have loved to have looked closer but she was too busy concentrating on not steering off the path into the water and reeds below. But it took her mind off Harry and she was glad of that. It wasn't her job to save the world. She plastered a smile on her face, determined to soak in the sun and the sensation of wind in her face and blow away the distractions of the man beside her.

Good. She looked happy again. Harry savoured Bonnie's uncomplicated enjoyment of the scenery and the people they passed, like a new-taste sensation. He rolled her spontaneity around in his mind like a sweet in his mouth. It had been too long since he'd felt those things and it swallowed the dark feelings he'd been left with.

But there was no escaping that through the course of today he'd begun to recognise that it wasn't healthy to stay as closed off from emotion as he'd been, so he noted her pleasure, learnt from it, and even began to question his isolation.

It hadn't all been escape here, though. A large part of Bali had been healing to his soul. He wished he could have shown her his mother's house. Let her feel the peace he always felt there. He wondered how she'd respond to that and to the different vibe of Ubud as a town.

He pedalled faster to catch her and when he was alongside he caught her eye. 'Will you have dinner with me tonight?' Funny how plans he formed for Bonnie were immediately acted on. Almost as if he acted before he could stop himself. Did he need more exposure when she was going? 'I'll drop you back at Kuta afterwards, and even take you to the airport tomorrow if you like.' The words just kept flying out. She was going. There was no offer of commitment in that.

Bonnie wanted to say yes. Knew she shouldn't because every minute she spent with this confusing and compelling guy meant he was going to be harder to leave behind when her plane took off.

She thought about Jimbaran, and the beach and all the people, and a secret place inside her whispered the urge to suggest somewhere more private, more amenable to intimacy, which should be the last thing she wanted. She was a fool. It was better to stay public. 'Tonight, yes, I'd like that. Not the airport tomorrow. I'll make my own way there.'

'As you wish,' he said, and she was glad. It was like a limit she'd set herself. So far but not all the way. Now, that had connotations she didn't want to think about.

'How about when the bus drops you off after the ride I'll pick you up in my car?' He glanced at her as if not sure how she'd react. 'Would you like to see Ubud? It's only an hour's run.'

She hesitated. She'd be agreeing to disappear into the middle of Bali with Harry. A man she hardly knew. But she was kidding herself if she thought she'd throw away the chance to spend a little more time with him before she had to leave.

And it seemed important to try to understand him before she left. Maybe even help him. 'Seems a long way to go for dinner.'

'Thought I'd show you my mother's house. We could catch a kekak dance or just have a quiet dinner overlooking the rice fields. I'd like you to see where I live and why I love it.'

She found herself agreeing, maybe foolishly, but the idea of being privy to a more personal side to Harry was too intriguing to resist. And she didn't want the day to end. This whole slice out of time would end soon enough, which was a good thing if she was going to get over being drawn to this often silent man, and why he was hiding here in Bali.

CHAPTER FIVE

LATER that afternoon, in Harry's car, Bonnie looked out the window as Harry drove.

Motorbikes were everywhere, swerving in and out of traffic, crazy loads piled on them, tooting politely to be let through. And nobody seemed cross.

Very different to Western cities she'd been to. She glanced at Harry as he slowed to allow a young biker to pass him, and he seemed lazily alert, not at all perturbed by the chaos. What was it about him that drew her to him? He was the opposite of her ex-fiancé, career-climbing Jeremy, which in the big picture should be a good thing.

Harry didn't seem driven by anything, foot-loose, fancy-free except for the ghost of a wife. Well, that was what she assumed. She hadn't actually asked him if he had a girlfriend but she didn't think so, he seemed content to just coast through life. He was unlike anyone she'd ever known or even been drawn to. Maybe that was the attraction.

The safety of him not being eligible in her eyes. And if she was honest, she was attracted to him despite her inner caution reminding her he was a man and men couldn't be trusted.

'Do you enjoy driving here?'

He grinned at her. Pure schoolboy without a care now. It must be nice to switch on and off like that. 'It's like the bargaining. Just smile and you'll be all right. Don't get worked up about anything and everything will run smoothly.'

Sounded like his life. 'Pleasantly detached in your bubble from the real world? Is that why you stay?'

He glanced at her and then away. 'Maybe.'

He changed the subject and she wasn't surprised. Right at the beginning he'd said there would be no deep and meaningful discussions.

'We're coming into Celuk. A village famous for silversmiths. I'd like to pick something up from a friend of mine.'

He slowed as they passed shopfronts and the occasional larger walled house, all proclaiming their trade in jewellery, and what woman didn't love jewellery? Bonnie was no exception as she turned her head from side to side to see the shop-fronts.

When they parked, almost against the wall to get off the narrow street, there was barely enough room to open her door, but that wasn't going to stop her having a peek inside.

Harry grinned again and helped her squeeze out onto the little porch and up the steps into the shop. To her delight the inside exceeded her ex-pectations. It seemed she'd found Aladdin's cave crammed to the ceiling with glass-fronted cup-boards packed with all types and sizes of silver jewellery.

He introduced her to his friend, Putu, who reached under the counter and produced a small box filled with silver charms. Putu poked around in the box until he found what he was looking for and offered it to Harry.

She couldn't see what it was and at first thought it some sort of animal as Harry held it up to the light. She watched him clap his friend on the back and some money exchanged hands. And she looked away to control her inquisitiveness. There were trays and trays of all types of silver jewellery, plenty to distract a curious woman.

Harry strode across to her. 'Sorry to keep you in the dark but I wanted Putu to find the best one.' He opened his hand. 'I'd like you to have this, a keepsake of today.' Harry stopped beside her and held out his palm. 'As an apology for being so stressed.'

There in the middle of his strong brown hand lay a tiny silver baby, curled up and content, beautifully crafted and cleverly suspended on a finely intricate chain.

'She's gorgeous,' she breathed, and looked from

Harry to the grinning shopkeeper. She could only marvel at the exquisite workmanship.

'In honour of your birth today.' He smiled and her legs wobbled in response. Good grief. She looked down at the shiny miniature again. Such dimpled cheeks and rounded limbs and something to remember Harry by. As if she'd forget him.

'Thank you, Harry.' She looked across at the silversmith and smiled. 'You're very clever.'

Harry stepped closer and, typically, all the hairs on her arms recognised him and stood up. She might even miss that sensation when she went. 'Here. Let me put it on for you.'

She turned and lifted her hair so he could fasten the clasp, and his fingers on her neck lifted any other follicle that wasn't upright already. She stepped back, ostensibly to thank the silversmith but really to loosen the tightness in her chest and mentally fan her face.

The shopkeeper brought the mirror and she could see herself with Harry behind her, like a picture. A picture that would soon become a memory.

She turned and impulsively reached up to kiss his cheek. 'Thank you. She's beautiful. I love her.' He patted her shoulder and turned away to hide the expression in his eyes, and she sighed.

Well, that had been a mistake. Harry briefly closed his eyes. He'd thought by buying her a trinket he could lose the guilt he still carried by not telling her the truth. But it hadn't worked.

Actually, he felt worse, almost as though he was trying to buy her forgiveness, which was ridiculous when, in fact, he owed nothing to this woman he barely knew. So why did he feel he was deepening the deceit?

Because when it was all said and done she'd go on her way in good faith, blithely unaware he should have stood beside her at the birth and been there to support her in the responsibility. And he hadn't.

He'd lied by omission, run away from the risk

of something going wrong, and pretended she had been the only person with the knowledge.

He helped her back into the car and ensured she had her seat belt on and wondered, as he climbed in himself, what the heck was he doing with her beside him at this moment?

Why hadn't he waved goodbye after the bike ride and chalked the new insights she'd given him up for later thought or consigned them to the too-hard basket like he usually did? He had no idea but he had the sneaking suspicion he was going to regret this decision.

He eased his vehicle back into the mayhem of the traffic and decided his mind was as bad as the street. Chaotic.

Bonnie took one look at Harry's set face and chose to stare out the window. She suppressed another sigh. The man was like a roller-coaster— exhilarating on the downward loops but full of unexpected corners that threatened to derail her when she least expected it.

She'd just concentrate on the scenery and the bustling life all around her.

When they arrived in Ubud the main street was packed with shops. Windows were filled with hand-printed clothes, paintings, imitation designer luggage. There seemed to be dozens of restaurants, lots to distract her confusion from Harry's behaviour.

As they passed the stone-walled palace she began to see that the centre of town was built on a mountain, complete with rainforest and plunging gullies, and lush foliage everywhere. A town nestled in a jungle.

Ubud had a different feel to the beachside suburbs and Bonnie was glad she'd had the chance to experience the variation. It had nothing to do with more time with the enigmatic Harry.

Serene women in yellow sashes carried towering arrangements of offerings on their heads up stone steps, and everywhere were the welcoming smiles of Bali.

She wished she could concentrate on the

colours and activity and sheer beauty around her, but despite her attempt at resistance her eyes were drawn to the man beside her.

Fascination lay in the way his brown hands moved confidently on the steering wheel, how easy he made it seem to navigate in the busyness and ordered confusion that was the main street, and how since they'd arrived in Ubud his shoulders seemed to have relaxed again into their more comfortable stance.

Her hand slid up to touch the baby around her neck. The gift had come from nowhere and she wasn't sure that he was happy now that he'd given it to her. But she couldn't read his face and maybe it would be better to let the distance grow between them again. She turned back to the window.

They crawled with the now-creeping traffic down a stone-banked incline then across an ancient bridge and suddenly the shops and traffic were gone and they were surrounded by rice fields again.

Harry bumped into a narrow lane and up another hill and the rice fields almost brushed the car. She assumed they must be getting closer to the time they'd arrive at his house and little waves of awareness bounced between them in the quiet of the car. Then he turned and smiled at her and it seemed it was connection time again.

The guy was such a light switch sometimes. On and off with the flick of a finger.

The suspense of their arrival became more momentous the longer it took to get there. She reminded herself he was a well-known entity here, and she wasn't really foolish sitting beside him going somewhere she didn't know how to get back from. The concept that Harry would force her into anything didn't enter her mind. She trusted him and she didn't know why. Just that she did.

Would anyone else be there? Was it only a peaceful dinner they were both thinking of or had thoughts of intimacy crossed his mind too?

Should she keep reminding herself she was a paranoid woman with a poor track record in men?

She sneaked a look at his profile as he glanced to his right. Hopefully he was unaware of the mixed emotions she was hiding behind her sunglasses because she couldn't keep her thoughts sorted and orderly herself, let alone share them with him.

Field workers waved and Harry waved back, and Bonnie gazed around and pretended to be the tourist she was, but her eyes kept returning to Harry's hands. The very first time she'd seen him she'd felt a connection to those hands—until she'd seen his ring. How ridiculous. You couldn't fall in lust with someone's hands.

They finally arrived, as close as they could get anyway. Harry's house was on a rise, white-painted stone and many gabled, with a veranda on every side. He couldn't drive all the way to the door so they walked up a stone path along the edge of a rice field and she could see ducks playing in the water that lay beneath the rice plants.

When he opened the gate for her she felt her own shoulders drop because, magically, the peace and tranquillity wrapped around them both from the first footstep into the gardens.

It was as if she'd stepped into a lush green veil of peace. Unexpected and very welcome. Harry rested his hand on the small of her back as she stood there and drank in the serenity, and even his presence became a part of the whole.

'No wonder you love it,' she said quietly, and shook her head at perfection. Brushed grass, tiled edges around gardens, little waterfalls and fountains, and a myriad of tiny stone altars with incense and frangipani flowers artfully arranged.

Harry sighed with relief. It had been right to bring her. 'Come inside.' He could feel the swell of pleasure that she could see what drew him to stay.

He saw it through her eyes, re-examining the facets he loved with renewed appreciation.

Stone steps flanked by granite lions led up to a magnificently tiled veranda that peered over a sheer drop to the valley floor. A long way down, like a silver ribbon, a small stream meandered along under the lush rainforest that lay in pockets between the layered rice fields.

Further along the veranda, on what seemed like acres of tiles, cushioned cane furniture waited patiently for a casual visitor to drop and soak in the scene below.

A feeling of closeness grew as she shared Harry's vision of his home. Like a window into a part of him that could help her understand him. 'Thank you for bringing me here, Harry. It's wonderful.'

A smiling Balinese man, perhaps in his sixties, approached with welcoming hands held out towards her. Harry spoke from behind her shoulder. 'Ketut, this is Miss Bonnie. She is a midwife and flies back to Darwin tomorrow.'

Ketut inclined his head and smiled warmly. 'Welcome, Miss Bonnie. It is with great pleasure I meet you. Come, sit, let me make you both tea after your journey.'

Well, that answered who else would be there, Bonnie thought, and stifled pathetic disappointment they wouldn't be alone. She remembered then that Harry had spoken of his mother's caretakers. She should have remembered.

'Hello, Ketut.' Bonnie settled into the luxurious cushions and raised her brows at Harry. She mouthed, *Wow* at the whole setting. 'Tea would be lovely. Thank you.' Ketut smiled and hurried away.

'I thought we'd have afternoon tea here.' Harry gestured to the view. 'You could look around after that and decide where you'd like to eat. If you'd rather come back here, we can let Ketut know in time for him to whip something up. He's a great cook.'

A busy restaurant was the last thing she wanted but she'd definitely be safer—from herself. Here, she knew she'd be tempted to peer through the cracks in the walls of Harry's isolation, to see why he affected her, why she worried about his inner sadness that he hid from the world but not from her, how she could help him. Every time she felt close to the answer in public he'd shut her out again and step back. Did she need that angst? Could she stop herself anyway? What if he did open up to her and they connected in a way that would hurt much more when she flew away tomorrow?

No, she didn't need that. 'We could go out. There's dozens of restaurants nearby. I'm easy.'

'No, you're not.' Harry watched her blink in surprise and her shock was ironic. He wasn't finding any of this girl/boy stuff easy when it concerned this woman. A notion all of his friends would find vastly amusing. 'But it's not your fault I find you difficult to fathom. Maybe I'm just out of practice.' He shrugged. 'But back to dinner. If you truly don't mind, let's eat here. We could walk the gardens. I'll show you the house and we can have drinks on the platform overlooking the valley. Ketut will be happy doing what he loves and we'll still drive through Ubud at night to show it to you when we leave to take you back to your hotel.'

She looked away to the river below as she tried to stay relaxed—or at least appear that way. Hard with her knee almost touching his as they sat side by side. Tension simmered like a pot of soup between them. Millions of tiny bubbles that surfaced beneath her skin as the heat of Harry increased. And there was the intimacy of the setting. His house. Foreign country. Alone except for the caretakers.

The mood settled when Ketut returned with fresh ginger tea and a gorgeous seed cake, but Bonnie laughed at them both when each rushed into speech as soon as Ketut left. 'You first...' Harry said.

Bonnie picked her cake up with forced enthusiasm, anything to break the awkwardness of the moment. 'I won't need dinner.'

Harry's glance warmed her. 'I want to feed you up before you go on the plane tomorrow.' That reminded them both she was going, until the direction of his gaze settled on her lips. She wished he wouldn't do that and she tried to concentrate on her imminent departure. His knee touched hers again, deliberately, and she felt more warmth sear through his jeans, the surge of intense awareness she would always associate with Harry. Not fair. Poor Jeremy had never been like this.

They looked at each other and it was as if invisible threads were looping and diving over each other in an intricate dance until she was encapsulated within a tapestry of secret knowledge they shared. Ridiculous. They shared nothing in common except today's experiences.

Her own gaze dropped to his mouth, those gorgeous lips she'd admired at Jimbaran, and she saw him smile, and just as quickly she blushed again. Harry stood up and she found herself beside him as he gathered her fingers into his hand and tugged her closer until her hip was touching his.

She moved into his arms as they stood together on his porch. Harry stared, unsmiling, down into her face and his eyes became deep royal blue, dark and promising, and she told herself it was because his pupils had dilated, a physiological event, not a revelation.

'I'd like to kiss you,' he murmured, his voice a physical caress.

Her heart tripped, stuttered and gathered speed. Her mouth dried. 'Why?'

He smiled with his eyes but still not his mouth. 'Because I think we'd both enjoy it.'

Lordy, yes. 'Oh.'

He leaned closer. At the last minute she closed her eyes, all the better to feel him with, and his mouth touched hers, gently. Homecoming—strange, when she'd never visited before. Like nothing she'd expected and much, much better.

He was the first man she'd kissed since Jeremy, and instead of the masculine assertion that had always left her backpedalling away in confusion, Harry held the notion of mastery back. She could still taste the edges of his intent but it was infinitely subtle. Subdued by patience, imbibed with the same sense of peace she'd felt as she'd come through his garden gate. She felt like she belonged here. In Harry's arms. And kissing as he allowed her to choose the pace.

A novel idea, and tentatively she opened her mouth and tilted her tongue to his. Just a flutter. His arms tightened around her, he made a tiny sound in his throat as he pulled her closer into his body, and her other hand drifted to encircle his neck of its own free will.

And so the kiss gradually deepened, evolved, ripened into something tangibly alive and nour-ishing and enriching to her soul. To both their souls, she decided as she pushed closer, suddenly unable to be hard enough against his chest. She sighed with the rightness and connection and joy she hadn't experienced before.

Then, with a premonition she hadn't expected, like the dampness of a sun shower, she felt the tears in her eyes, a poignancy of devastation to come for when it must end, and that thought gave the connection a heartrending simplicity she could barely endure.

It seemed Harry's arms were a place she'd been searching for and never known she'd missed, and when he gently withdrew, as warned, she was bereft.

How to hide what she'd just discovered? She stepped back and turned away and behind her back she could feel the wall rise between them—not surprising for two fort dwellers—and no doubt Harry's closed expression mirrored hers.

This was dangerous and foolhardy for a woman only just recovered from a broken heart. How could she have been so stupid?

'Maybe that wasn't such a good idea,' he murmured. She turned back, her face mostly under control, the tears wiped away surreptitiously. He smiled with his mouth this time, but not his eyes, no humour in his face. She knew just how he felt. 'Perhaps I should show you the house and grounds?'

She nodded, and they walked into the house,

but again he captured her hand and she didn't want him to let her go.

The afternoon was surreal after that. The house seemed spread over many levels; because of the hillside, it floated up and down between rooms. Floated like the aura that floated between them.

Each window and landing gave space and light and vibrant exposure to the lime of the rice fields or the shininess of the tropical foliage. Each window beckoned like the heat that was building between them.

Furnishings, fountains and secluded benches in lush green nooks in the gardens all served as a backdrop for just one more kiss. Nothing more, no huge urgency, which in itself seemed surreal when they both knew their time together was ending.

One more lean into Harry's shoulder. One more stroke of his hand down her back. Both pretending the day wasn't going to end and talking of things not of the future and not of the past but of their inner thoughts. Music, books, morals.

As the afternoon lengthened, so did the kisses. The embraces became more intense, a slow build of fever was upon them like a tropical malady that had only one cure. And slowly, surely, inescapably, they finally drifted to the house and the master bedroom.

The huge four-poster with its snow-white mosquito net draped above seemed to smile at them. Dark, Balinese carved furniture stood like nodding sentries around them as he sat her down on the edge of the bed and stared into her eyes.

Bonnie knew she shouldn't be there, could see the risk of regret that tomorrow could bring her, the whisper of the voice of reason warning her she would lament her weakness, but this was all she could give. This wasn't weakness, this was strength. Her healing gift to Harry.

Bonnie couldn't leave him suspended, marking time, when he should move on. She didn't know why she felt she had the power to change that. That she was the one who could help battle his demons and ease his fear of more damage to his soul.

The tears tightened behind her eyes and her chest ached for him—this man who had broken through her defences with frightening ease— ached for his broken heart she wanted to mend.

But what about hers? This was crazy, and dangerous, and guaranteed to hurt later, but then, so would not being there with Harry. Not doing this. Harry had so many demons, and hers had flown—she wasn't sure when but she felt gloriously free.

Such was irony, that thought flitted away with the next kiss and the feel of him against her. Still he held her hand, as if he'd never let her go, and she allowed the fantasy its rein as they lay down fully clothed and began to kiss again. They could no more stop kissing than stop breathing. It was as if they both knew it was their last chance.

Kisses so tender, so sweet. Kisses that tugged at her very soul. She could feel the beat of his heart, thumping under the solid wall of his chest against hers, pumping faster as his kisses deepened, his need building, matching her own rising need until she too was breathless. Burning, aching, then suddenly afraid.

She should be afraid. The thought drifted in and out of her sensation-filled mind, afraid of him, afraid of herself and her own body she suddenly knew so little about, consequences, her body that was at the same time so innocent and yet so wanton.

Harry drew away, lifted his mouth from hers, stroked her cheek, and searched her face for a change of heart—again he'd read her mind and answered her unspoken plea like he had earlier that day—and she knew she had only to shake her head and he would hold her gently and be still.

And so the fear drifted away. Disappeared in the blue of his eyes and the understanding she could feel in her soul. How could this be wrong?

Now there was no fear. Only the knowledge that this was right. Nothing could be more right.

And when they came together, their hearts beat in time, just as their bodies entwined like the vines outside the window.

Somehow it had become her goal to free him from his past. Her one focus to make him see how beautiful the world was and that he was allowing it to pass. She knew in her soul he was too good a man to leave like this and in that way she could never regret her gift to him—or his to her.

Afterwards he held her, dried her tears of joy, whispered his own amazement, kissed her eyelids and smoothed her hair.

Eventually, after much gentle teasing and quests of discovery, they showered together in the tiled room off the master bedroom with the window wide-open to the now empty fields. The workers would be home with their families; the birds too seemed to have settled.

The afternoon closed towards evening and they drifted toward the set table, 'Will you come back?' he asked, and the reality of her leaving eased between them like a third person.

'We'll see.' And they both knew that was a no. Yes, she was leaving. Tomorrow and a huge ocean and an even huger land mass would be between them. She'd glimpsed that spending more time with Harry would make her miss him more and she was almost glad she wouldn't have the chance. There was no future for them and she didn't want to regret what they'd had.

Perilously, they'd felt too right for people who would never fit their lives together, so no false promises had been made or exchanged. And that was right too. But he would always hold a place in her heart, as she hoped she would have in his.

Somewhere inside both of them peace remained.

Dinner was served on the veranda, two seats side by side, hips touching, and strangely there was no awkwardness between them to ruin the enjoyment of the colours of the approaching night and the last minutes of their time together.

Ketut had prepared a palate of ginger salad and garlic prawns with nasi goreng, everything redolent of the fresh coriander the Balinese loved. Everything tasted good. Shone brighter, smelt divine.

For Harry the last of the afternoon sun slipped away from an amazing day, a day of birth, warmth and approaching goodbyes from this woman who had tilted his world in a new direction. Perhaps because all those issues lay beneath their conversations they finally talked a little about the past and themselves. Though Bonnie found it easier to be open than he did.

She spoke of the nursing positions she'd held in the Outback. He'd seen the places, finally mentioned them but not in the context of the work he still kept from her, that he'd had flown in and out of them and for the first time in a long time a tiny stirring of regret for that life flickered in him.

He almost told her of Steve's offer. Confessed he was the medic who didn't show. His fault she had to leave early. But he didn't. Uluru was too close to the township of Katherine where Clara had died and already he'd compromised himself. The beginnings of shame for all he hadn't told her began to colour his evening.

'If you come to Bali again, I could show you more she has to offer.'

Bonnie narrowed her eyes at him. 'You never know the future but I hope you won't be here if I ever come back. I don't know what you're hiding from, Harry, but I hope you'll have decided to move on and do something kinder to yourself.'

Harry blinked. Nobody spoke to him like that. She was nothing if not forthright. 'Or you could come back,' he said.

'Or you could move on. Don't waste your life, Harry.'

He could have spoken of his mother's friend and how she'd started a birth centre for the women of the village. Those who couldn't afford to pay for a midwife in Ubud.

He knew she'd love that. How before his marriage he'd worked there several months a year, and loved it. How the ex-pats now used it as well because of the women-centred care they could have that so opposed the medically orientated care they would otherwise receive. But he'd not been back to the centre since Clara's death.

'Thank you for the day, Harry. It's been lovely.' She glanced at her watch, briefly touched his hand on the table and then stood up. Ketut appeared from the dimness.

Bonnie shook hands with Ketut. 'Thank you for a wonderful dinner.'

'You must come back.' Ketut slanted a glance at Harry who, to Bonnie's eyes, avoided the older man's suggestion.

'Maybe one day,' she said, and gathered her bag.

When they'd walked along the rice field path, she turned once more to look up at his house and it seemed so natural to have her hand in Harry's. 'It's been a magical afternoon and evening. Thank you.'

Harry helped her into the car. 'Thank you,' he said, but he was feeling more than a little battered. He wasn't sure what had possessed him to allow this woman as close as he had or why he'd broken his rule and brought her to his house. Let alone opened himself up and then kissed her like a hungry schoolboy and whisked her off to bed like a one-night stand. Of course, there had been an amazing connection he hadn't been prepared for. He'd been telling himself how dangerous she was since he had first laid eyes on her. Not a good choice. And ramifications he'd pay for later when he couldn't sleep.

Imagine if they hadn't been careful. He had a sudden vision of Bonnie with his child and the fear leapt into his throat like a rabid dog. He'd known her two days and pictures of disaster there were such that he knew he'd never recover from them. Thank goodness they'd been sensible there at least. Both of them.

It was deeply fortunate she was about to get on a plane and fly away. He'd never met anyone like her. Didn't understand how she could be so forthright, even hard on him, one minute and so giving the next. Perhaps it was the fact that she didn't think of herself when she gave and that shattered him. Her selfless generosity.

The drive to her hotel was accomplished with little of the usual traffic delay and all too soon she was turning to face him with her room key in her hand.

'Thank you for bringing me home, Harry.'

What could he say? She'd turned his life upside down in forty-eight hours. 'Thank you for spending your time with me.'

She stepped into his arms and it was his turn to close his eyes as he hugged her to him. He rested his chin on the top of her head for a moment and breathed in the vanilla scent of her hair that was already painfully familiar. Soaked in the feel of her against his chest, all soft, yet supple, a little too thin, and painfully dear already. He was mad, standing here ready to hurt as soon as she moved.

She pulled away and looked up into his face. Then she reached up and kissed him. Light and fleeting—like her. 'Goodnight, Harry. Look after yourself.' Then she turned round and walked quickly away.

'You too,' he said to her back.

The next morning Bonnie's suitcases needed only closing, and there were still two hours to go before her bus to the airport. Sweat trickled down her back as she sat by the pool in her sarong and swimmers with her book as she tried to block out the idea of any chance of seeing Harry. It would only be worse.

The tiny movement at the corner of her eye spun like a coin into a wishing well, a flicker of light as she turned the page of her novel. Bonnie blinked, looked around, not sure what she'd seen—maybe a thrown toy or the kick from an underwater swimmer—but the unease she felt made her drop her book and jog to the edge of the pool just to check.

A crescent of shadow lay on the bottom, one without movement and immeasurably gut-wrenching. Bonnie dived into the pool still wearing sarong and sunglasses just as a woman screamed.

By the time she surfaced with a limp toddler in her arms a crowd had gathered, and the child was lifted from her arms, then she too was pulled from the pool by willing hands.

'Someone, call an ambulance.' The woman who'd lifted the child from her glanced at the toddler's staring eyes and lack of movement and Bonnie saw panic flare in her face. Her face screwed up and she pushed the child into Bonnie's hands and walked away quickly—and left Bonnie to cope by herself.

Bonnie glanced around. For a moment she thought she saw Harry but then an old man stopped in front of her and she realised it was wishful thinking because nobody seemed willing to help her.

She sank to the ground with the child in her arms and jammed down the panic that would only make it harder. She didn't bother to check for a pulse before she puffed two small mouthfuls of air into the child's lungs. Then she shifted and began cardiac compressions, counting quietly as she strove to block out the people crowding to look but not to help.

The elderly gentleman knelt down beside her, his blue-veined hands shaking as he clasped them together. 'I don't know how to help. What do you want me to do?'

'Can you do mouth-to-mouth? Little puffs. I'll do the chest compressions, that's the most important. Watch me. I'll show you.' She shifted quickly and puffed two small puffs until the little chest rose and fell. Then she moved back to the side. 'Is anyone a doctor?' Bonnie said shortly, and glanced around at the bystanders.

'Anyone at all?' She began to count out loud

again as her fingers found the child's sternum and began to compress on the little chest with cardiac massage. She shook her head when no one spoke.

'Twenty-eight, twenty-nine, thirty…' Bonnie paused, shifted again to breathe twice. The little chest rose and fell, and Bonnie looked across at the older man. 'Can you do that?'

His eyes filled with tears. 'I don't think so.'

'Watch the clock for me, then, please.' She started again.

Harry's brain screamed to help but he couldn't move. He saw the old man shake his head and that was the moment Harry pushed his way through. He pushed not just through the people but the wall of fear that sucked the breath from his chest. Wrestled himself free from the giant steel claws that had held him back from the first moment he'd realised what was going on—the powerful memories of another dead baby he had worked on had been too strong.

His non-compliant feet hadn't moved, despite

his brain urging them on, and his heart had thumped in his chest like it was going to explode. Then he'd felt relief as the older gentleman had joined her. He didn't need to get involved. They'd be fine.

But seconds later he'd seen the old man's shake of the head and Bonnie had looked up in desperation as she'd been left to her own resources again. Finally he'd been able to break the hold on his limbs and thrust himself forward. He hoped he wasn't too late.

Bonnie felt panic rising again as the little girl continued to lie flaccid beneath her. Then suddenly Harry, of all people, dropped down beside her to help. 'I'll do the compressions. I know what I'm doing.'

He compressed the toddler's chest. There was no hesitation, exactly a third in depth, no over- or under-compensation, which spoke of years of practice, and she shelved the questions that surfaced bitterly until she had time. Please, God, such precision would squeeze the little heart to force oxygen to the child's brain. In that captured moment, with the shock of the threat of death for this child a reality, for a split second in time as he cradled the child's chest Bonnie was struck by the snapshot of Harry's hands, hands she hoped she could trust with a child's life.

She breathed two breaths as the thirty-second mark came around again. 'Are you medical?'

'A doctor.' He didn't look at her. 'You must have seen her fall in. How long was she under for?'

'Twenty-eight, twenty-nine, thirty.' Bonnie paused, breathed twice, the little chest rose and fell, and Bonnie looked up at the old man. 'How's the time, please?' She started again.

'One and a half minutes.' How long had he been there? But that wasn't important. Why wasn't the little one responding?

The next half a minute dragged with aching slowness, thirty chest compressions, two breaths. Then another thirty seconds.

'Come on,' Harry muttered after Bonnie's next breaths and he compressed again, and as he finished speaking the tiny girl blinked slowly and finally screwed up her face before she coughed and began to cry weakly.

Bonnie felt a sob catch in her throat, the sudden heat of tears mixed with the swimming-pool water that still trickled down her face from her hair, and a huge shudder rippled down her back. She looked at Harry and no doubt her own relief was reflected in his eyes as he stared back at her.

Then raw ache at the back of her throat as she held back the sob continued to grow in size like a sharp rock in her neck and she pulled back out of the way as Harry rolled the little girl onto her side and into the recovery position.

She heard him say, 'Thank God,' as she inched further away. It had been him she'd seen. Why had he waited? Then the traumatised mother threw herself down beside her daughter and burst into tears. The sound of a distant ambulance siren drifted across the pool area.

Bonnie kept retreating until she could slip unnoticed back to her chair to retrieve her handbag.

Her sarong had ripped, the wet fabric ungiving as she'd flung herself down, and she just wanted to hide somewhere and curl up after the near horror. She bit the skin of one hand to stop the chatter of her teeth as she felt shock well inside her.

A Balinese waitress approached diffidently and held out her wet sunglasses.

Bonnie met her eyes. There, too, huge tears trickled in mutual horror and dawning relief of the child regaining consciousness. 'Thank you.' The little waitress could barely make her words form. 'To lose a child would harm our souls for ever.'

Bonnie sucked in air. 'We're all very lucky.'

The little waitress inclined her head. 'Fortunate to have you, and the doctor.' They both looked across to where Harry's face was like granite as he stood with the little girl in his arms. He glanced up as if saying that had been too close.

The anguish in his face made the rock in her throat return. It had been him she'd glimpsed at the start. But surely not? However, when she replayed in her mind that image she knew it was true. Why hadn't he come straight away? Why had he left her alone when she'd needed him? Why had he not mentioned he was a doctor in the last two days? A man she'd shared special time with, a birth with, made love with. That was what liars did.

'I need to go to my room.' Bonnie tried to smile at the waitress but all she could think of was that she needed to get away before she broke down.

She saw him glance her way, saw him read the distress in her eyes. Harry was hurting too but she didn't care. He'd left her to cope on her own. He'd lied to her from the moment they'd met. The picture burned in her brain as she walked blindly to her room.

Like the last man she'd dared to care about.

Yes, she'd been very glad he'd been there at the end but would never understand his hesitation. He was a doctor and he'd lied over and over again to her.

By the time Harry walked out of the hospital

in Denpasar an hour and a half later, the pain lashed him in a hundred places he'd forgotten— and none of them were physical.

He'd stayed fairly immune during the drive in the ambulance. The little girl, Ginger, had been awake and croakily stable but he'd been unable to leave her until she was safely in hospital and monitored by experienced personnel.

But walking out that hospital door into the stickiness of the Balinese heat, the memories hit him like a car full of tourists.

He'd done okay today, thanks mostly to Bonnie, but how was he to live with the crushing guilt of his delay in response?

It had happened in his first emergency after Clara had died. His colleagues had told him it was only natural, to give himself time, but he'd backed away in horror. A man not to be trusted. A doctor unable to deal with emergencies. A man ashamed of a vocation that had been his life. So he had run to Bali.

Avoided any contact with medicine. And

drifted. Drifted until a determined little midwife had dragged him into the very situation he'd been running from.

That was why he'd vowed he didn't want people's lives in his hands. Especially those of babies. Imagine if the little one had died.

That was why he stayed here. In the furore he hadn't apologised to Bonnie for not helping earlier. Being catatonic with fear, allowing others to do what he could have done better, was no excuse, and no doubt she despised him. Well, that was okay. He despised himself. He knew he was far from perfect. He just hadn't realised how far.

But there, in the back of his tortured mind, was the glimmer of a chance to explain. He could probably catch her at the airport if he left now but he didn't know what to say to her if he found her. But could he let her fly away without telling her why? And she'd need to debrief, if only a little. He was an expert in what happened if you didn't do that.

In the end it was Bonnie who found him. He'd

been leaning up against a pylon in the departure hall when she'd walked past, dragging her suitcase.

She glanced sideways, saw him, jerked her bag a little as if to decide whether to stop or not, when Harry straightened.

'Hello, Bonnie.' Lord she was beautiful to him. She looked stressed, which wasn't surprising; she looked upset, which was his fault; and she looked confused about whether she was glad to see him or not. He supposed he could be thankful for that small mercy.

He met her eyes. 'I don't know what to say.'

She tightened her hand on the bag. 'Luckily that's your problem, not mine, Harry.'

He ran his hand through his hair and sighed. 'I'm sorry, Bonnie.'

She lifted her head. 'For which thing? Lying for the last two days or not helping me save a child's life until it was almost too late?'

He deserved that. 'All of it. And there are reasons for both.'

She shook her head. A physical denial. 'Well, don't try to explain because the excuse won't be good enough.' She glanced up at the clock. 'I have a plane to catch and I'm already late.' She put her hands up to her neck and undid the clasp on the necklace. 'I'd rather not keep this.' She dropped the little silver baby on a chain into his hand and jerked her bag. Then the words flew out as if she couldn't prevent them. 'How dare you lie to me? All this time.'

He closed his fingers over the charm and sighed. 'I lost my wife. My unborn child. I can't do medicine any more. I can't talk about it.'

She tossed her hair. 'Maybe you should because I can't see hiding it is doing you any good.'

'My choice.'

Brittle emerald, her eyes were like temple stones as she glared at him. 'I don't think you should have that choice. Lives are lost, Harry. Medicine isn't run by God. We do the best we can and sometimes our best isn't good enough.

'It's hard, but if every skilled doctor, every

trained practitioner reared away from that reality, if they all turned their backs selfishly on their vocations like you have while you were buried here, how many more families have to feel that same sense of loss before you help?'

She tossed her hair and he could read the hurt in her face. 'There was almost another family today. How do you feel about that?'

He shouldn't have come. This wasn't doing either of them any good. 'It can't be my problem. I can't be calm like you were.'

That sobered the fury in her head. He saw it drain away and be replaced by pity. Pity he didn't want. 'You missed the nausea episode in my room that followed after I left the pool area. I wasn't so calm then.'

He heard her but it wasn't the same. She'd responded instantly to the situation. He didn't have that faith in himself. 'You were calm when it mattered and that's a big part of why that mother still has her child.'

Then he saw it in her eyes. Her own doubt and

fear about a situation that wasn't so different from his—except she hadn't given in to it.

It was a lightning bolt of perception. Bonnie could choose not to admit the fear if she was unable to save the child, not give in to the helplessness of being alone in that emergency. The way he had. He never used to be like that. He'd been the first on the scene, the fastest with treatment. The golden boy of the Royal Flying Doctor Service. The bigger they are, the harder they fall.

Now he'd let her down. Continued to let himself down.

Then she lifted her head. 'Do you know how the little girl is?'

Her most important question. At least he could answer that for her. 'No ill effects so far. I just left the hospital.'

'Good!' She even smiled, not at him but into the air with relief, and he was glad about that. In itself it was validation of standing here feeling like hell. That smile made it worth it.

'Now I'm going,' she said, and he felt a slam

of desolation he hadn't expected. At least he'd tried to explain. She pulled the bag forward a few inches and then stopped. 'You should give medicine another go, Harry. You might find salvation instead of hell. You never know. But if you ever want to talk about it, don't come and find me.'

Harry watched her disappear into the departure area and then turned away, but her accusations haunted him. Accusations he didn't want to think about. Was he egotistical and self-absorbed? He would have said self-protective. Or was it just the thought of practising medicine that jerked him into denial?

It was as well he hadn't had more time before her flight left because he didn't know what he would have been capable of to try and talk her into staying just a little longer. To try to explain.

What was she saying? What did she mean? That someone else could have been there to help him when he'd lost his own baby? Someone like him, turning his back? Like Steve and that short-term job at the Rock and his own refusal to go?

He couldn't do it. Or could he? He'd managed with the baby but that had been a close thing. Could he go back to diagnoses and the mistakes that left him open to self-recrimination?

Then again, could he not? Life was looking pretty damn empty right at this moment.

During the drive back to Ubud, Harry noticed things he hadn't seen for a long time. Things Bonnie had pointed out to him with excitement.

He saw the families, crammed on motorbikes, children sitting on bags of grain behind their fathers, mums balancing their two-wheeled pick-ups as if it was the most normal thing in the world to carry a table on a motor bike.

It had always been this way as the motorcycle could be afforded and the car not, and suddenly to Harry it seemed incredibly alien to see babies, cradled by their precariously squashed mothers, jammed onto scooters between husbands and other children.

The small trucks packed with workers in the back; the Indonesian signage and waving palm trees were suddenly more visible. And here he was, pretending to be a part of it all when, in fact, he was really a bystander. An isolated one too scared to be involved in his own world where he belonged.

Harry's world was in turmoil and Bonnie had done it. Bonnie and a little girl now safe in her mother's arms.

Bonnie had been there when he'd been screaming inside, *This baby's going to die too*, the scene fraught with emotion. An unwanted return to a situation he'd chosen to avoid, and now where was he? Apart from profoundly appreciative of her calm in an emergency, maybe it was the frailty of a toddler's breathing and the fact that he and Bonnie had skills to save a life that had him thinking.

Or maybe it was just Bonnie who was attracting these medical disasters. He'd managed to avoid them for the last year. He'd known her three days and they'd had two already.

He saw his life, drifting from one leisurely Balinese day to the next, focused on the small issues, never thinking of the large ones in case it made him aware of what he'd chosen to discard in his fear of being hurt again.

Maybe he did need a dose of Bonnie McKenzie's reality to kick him back into gear. Bonnie would certainly give him that but he couldn't face the thought of a hospital, even the slightly slower paced one in Darwin, impersonally rushing from one patient to the next. And he wasn't ready for the commitment of general practice.

The Royal Flying Doctor Service was always looking for staff but even in the state he was in he could see how frustrating it would be to fly everywhere wondering when next he'd get to Uluru and a certain straight-talking midwife.

That was the crunch. He needed to see if what he suspected was true. Needed to see if Bonnie was the key to a normal world. Nothing more than that because he wasn't doing the family thing again. Wasn't going there. But it still left a lot they could share. If she was interested.

But would she be happy to see him drop out of the central Australian sky into Uluru? He knew Steve would. If he hadn't found a replacement yet.

The acceleration as the wheels left the ground pushed Bonnie back in her seat. She closed her eyes then opened them again to watch the land fall away beneath her. Better to face reality after all her harsh words to Harry to do the same.

She looked out. That would be Jimbaran Bay there and she could almost smell the smoke from the barbecues on the beach.

Harry St Clair. Another liar. A doctor hiding from the world in a web of lies. She couldn't believe she'd allowed him into her heart.

And she'd done that for sure. How could it ever have seemed inevitable at the time? But she couldn't deny, at unexpected moments, there'd been a real connection between them. But she would not give her heart to a man she couldn't trust and he'd wiped out that possibility for ever. She'd have her heart back if it killed her.

The Harry St Clairs weren't ready for the world and she was.

Now she had to let their time recede like the island somewhere below the aircraft wing. Bali would always be a place of memories and moments of gold and a man who wasn't who she'd thought, and she doubted she'd ever forget him. But she'd never go back.

Enough. It was time to do what she was good at. Getting on with life.

CHAPTER SIX

BONNIE drove into Uluru an hour before darkness fell. All the other cars seemed to be heading out of the township in a mass exodus, off to see the sunset, like the tourists did when they hit the beach in Bali. Of course, thinking of sunset swamped her with the uncomfortable memory of a certain tall widower and that last sunset in Ubud. Had it only been two days ago?

She dragged her mind away from Indonesia and remembered her friend in Darwin telling her about the ritual of sunset at Uluru.

A motorbike pulled out in front of her and she swerved to miss the suspiciously young Aboriginal couple running late for nature's best show. The boy waved and grinned and she saw his girlfriend was pregnant, heavily so, and that too reminded her of Bali. A precariously loaded motorbike and cheekily happy faces.

'Slow down, buddy, or you'll miss more than the sunset,' she muttered, but her mind was stuck like a piece of grass stuck in a Balinese water buffalo's hide.

She'd promised herself she wouldn't regret immersing herself in the Harry St Clair experience but that hadn't happened. She'd been in way over her head and spent the flight back trying to place at what moment good sense had escaped her. Hadn't she learned her lesson? The men she seemed attracted to were not to be trusted. She must have a homing device that attracted compulsive liars.

On the positive side, she hadn't once felt that inertia and sadness she'd felt since Jeremy's desertion and deceit. She was too angry.

Even though she'd found another man to let her down, somewhere in the mix, maybe a little to do with the Balinese beliefs, she did feel alive. Angry, but alive.

Harry's main deceit was to himself and until he addressed that he'd never be whole. She couldn't help him and she needed to concentrate on helping herself.

Her car eased slowly along the curved road past the hotel and she slowed as her eye was drawn to the uninterrupted views across the red sand hills to the great monolith in the distance.

Like a sleeping dinosaur, but millions of years older, Uluru showed its age in wrinkles of stone that caught and held the last of the sun's rays in textured lines of light and dark orange, and she could feel the rise of goose flesh in an unexpectedly primitive response to nature's spiritual beauty.

She hadn't expected that.

It was as if she suddenly began to feel the earth beneath her feet again, to be able to enjoy the beauty of her first sunset and each new place in a way she'd been too stressed and rushed to do in the last year while she'd dealt with Gran's slow death.

She flicked her mind away from the pull of the past and soaked in the new territory that would be hers to watch over.

Bonnie picked up her speed a little as she drove past a famous five-star resort with huge white sunshades soaring above the grand marble entry. The sort of place the Harrys of this world would stay.

Then she passed bungalows and an open-plan shopping centre and finally reached the neat and tidy medical centre nestled in its own block beside a small ambulance and police station, all the buildings lined up like a child's play village.

A lot of thought had gone into the planning of the township, the centre at the centre, she thought musingly as she pulled into the parking area out front.

Bonnie turned the car off and rolled her shoulders back into her seat. It had been a slow drive on the back way from Alice Springs, but she'd enjoyed the scenery. Taken her time, admired the meteor crater at Gosses Bluff, seen Kings

Canyon and gazed in amazement at flat-topped Mount Conner in the distance.

She'd had a close shave with a couple of big kangaroos as the long day had shifted into late afternoon, and it was good to get her battered Jeep here safely.

When she pushed open the door to the office the blast of cold airconditioning washed over her face like a cool sponge and she couldn't help a further lift in her spirits.

New jobs were always a challenge but today it was a stimulation she was keen to relish. Especially today. Three months out here at the centre of Australia promised to be an intriguing addition to her portfolio and the perfect antidote to holiday disillusionment.

'Can I help you?' The small, impeccably made-up woman at the desk looked a little incongruous compared to the patients ranged around the room, mostly ebony-skinned Aboriginal men and women with a scattering of red-faced tourists.

The receptionist had a lacy blouse that showcased her trim arms and light tan, shirts like

Bonnie had seen everywhere in Bali two days ago, like she herself had been wearing when she'd said goodbye to Harry on the way to her plane.

Bonnie shook off the thought. Okay already. She'd moved on. 'I'm Bonnie McKenzie, the new nurse practitioner. I start tomorrow.'

'Welcome. I'm Vicki.' She gestured to her badge. 'Receptionist.' Then she indicated a small doorway into a passage. 'My husband, Steve, is the practice manager here.'

She stood up. 'We're pleased to have you. Thanks for coming a couple of days early. Steve's still trying for a temporary doctor for the month we can't fill, and I'm starting to wonder if we'll ever get a permanent one.'

Vicki shrugged and then rolled her eyes. 'And the nurse you work with had to leave early because of an illness in her family. She'll be back next week, maybe.'

Vicki shrugged ruefully. 'Come through and I'll find Steve.'

Bonnie kept her face serene but her heart

dipped a little. It didn't look like she'd be getting much of an orientation if the medical staff were all away. Still, at least the ambos were next door and the practice manager would have first-aid training. Think *challenge*, she told herself, and fixed her enthusiastic smile in place with a new determination.

'Steve. The new sister is here.' Vicki gestured to an athletic-looking man, probably a couple of years older than Harry, who had the kindest eyes Bonnie had seen for a long time. Suddenly she felt better.

Bonnie nodded, and she suddenly remembered that people in the Outback preferred to nod, unlike their city counterparts, who were used to brushing up against people in crowded streets. 'Pleased to meet you, Steve.'

'And you too, Bonnie.' He looked fondly at his wife. 'Has Vicki told you we're it at the moment?'

'So she said. As long as I can find everything, I'm sure I can help. There's always the option of shipping people out.'

'Spoken like a trouper.' He gestured for her to precede him further along the narrow hallway. 'I'll show you around.'

The building was small but efficient, two consultation rooms, a long nurse's desk in front of four beds with curtains, and a sterilising and stock room. The computers were state-of-the-art and the practice guidelines were on prominent display. It was starting to feel familiar already.

Bonnie had done postings at Kununurra and Broome in Western Australia, as well as two small Aboriginal community postings, and her last four months in Darwin had been mostly maternity.

'So how many ambulance officers next door?'

Steve and Vicki exchanged smiles. 'That would be zero. There's just you driving until the nurse comes back. And maybe our doc if we get one. If you need to be in the back for transport, then Steve and I can both drive out to meet you.'

Oh, goody, Bonnie thought ruefully. She could just see herself haring off into the night in an ambulance to a car accident with the sirens blaring—out into the desert by herself. Now she wanted to ring her friends to come and play with her here.

'But hopefully you'll have backup, though we try only to work our doctors during office hours. It's so hard to get them here, we have to nurture them.'

Poor baby doctors. Bonnie fought to keep her eyebrows from scraping her hairline. She wasn't sure she succeeded. So nurses were more expendable. Mmm.

'So who are the people in the waiting room seeing?'

Vicki answered. 'Us. They're here for blood tests—people on heparin, insulin, stuff like that. Steve and I both take blood and we can do quick tests and send samples to be flown out on the afternoon plane for more complex results.'

'So these are all routine tests for regulars who have regimes printed out for them?'

'That's right. And the results are sent to the

flying doctor, who changes any medications they need.'

That sounded efficient, and not something they needed her for. Maybe she would get to find her bed and settle in before she started tomorrow. 'So, where do I stay?'

'The staff from the hotels, the clinics and even the tourist companies like pilots and guides all stay in the staff village. If you keep on the road you came in on, the village is down the third road on the left. You're in the Desert Pea Villas, room two, and the doctor is next door. The other nurse, Cleo, is upstairs, and Steve and I are along the corridor a little in five.'

It all sounded pretty simple. And a little too close for someone who liked their privacy and space, but she'd cope.

It rained torrentially in the night. Not a common occurrence at Uluru, and the hollows in the rock filled with water from myriad waterfalls off the enormous face. The waterfalls made small puddles and not so tiny pools in undulations where the hollows occurred.

Bonnie woke before dawn and the first thing she saw, the gecko on the ceiling above her head, reminded her of Bali.

Great! She threw back the covers and sat up, forced herself to feel her feet on the cool floor and grounded herself in the present—away from the memories of dinner on the beach at Jimbaran and rides through the rice paddies with a smiling Harry.

A plan had formed last night when she hadn't been able to sleep to walk one of the base sections of Uluru before sunrise. Her phone would keep her in contact, and that would clear her head for the day. The plan sounded even better now. She pulled on her clothes.

The drive to Uluru parking area beside the rock was accompanied by a gradual lightening of the sky to grey and finally to a faint glow of orange that promised a spectacular sunrise on the other side. Not that she'd see that with this great hulking monolith between her and the sunrise when she parked her vehicle, but this morning she wanted to get closer and actually touch the face. She'd dreamt of it through the night and the thought promised an inner calm she looked forward to.

As she crossed the car park she gazed in awe at the steepness of the actual climb to the top of the rock, steel posts and chains anchored to the almost vertical places on the accent face reached up to the pinkening sky above. Bonnie shook her head. No wonder some climbers had come to grief. It looked daunting and lonely, just her and none of the tourists still on the other side, awaiting the sun.

But it was awe-inspiringly beautiful. Wow. Her feet crunched in the sandy gravel as she crossed the deserted forecourt and followed the path to the base. It was cool beneath this giant shadow.

She kept left and finally the path snaked beside sheer cliffs and she could touch it. Lay her hand over the rough granules of time beneath her fingers and rest it there against the Rock's cool heartbeat. She had a sudden thought of Harry and whether he'd seen this. Felt this. What it would be like to share this with him.

The eerie sensation made her wonder whether the sight and feel and vibration of past eons would heal him too as she could feel the last of the walls inside her crumble and break into small particles of debris within her. Then she made him disappear like sand through her fingers because he threatened her new-found peace. She wandered alongside the sleeping beast for the next fifteen minutes before she turned back towards her car.

Shooting in and out amongst the scooped-out rock waterholes were pretty finches with scarlet upper feathers that were most noticeable when they were in flight. Firetails. She only recognised them because there was a shiny nature print above her bed with a close-up of the very same birds.

She wished she had someone—*like Harry, maybe*, a dissident voice inside suggested—to share her new knowledge with. No—of course not. But it would be fun to recognise more than one of the species of bird around here and she promised herself she'd buy a book on local fauna. Who needed company for that?

Suddenly she wanted the distraction of work and hastened her footsteps towards her car.

By the time she'd driven back, showered and had breakfast it would be nearly time for work. It had been an eventful morning already and no doubt the day held more interest yet.

It turned out well. Her morning left her with barely time to think let alone be distracted by memories. Patients with heat stroke, and knee scrapes that needed washing and cleaning, a fractured wrist and an eye full of sand, and Bonnie's last patient for the morning, a pale lady, Iris Wilson, who'd apparently already fainted in the waiting room.

Iris wasn't happy with the conditions of the Out-back.

'I'm not used to this heat. And I'm especially not used to the flies.' She shuddered delicately and looked ready to faint again. 'I'm terribly afraid I've swallowed one.'

Bonnie helped her to sit but before she could enquire, Iris rushed on. 'One of the dirty insects flew straight into my mouth and before I knew it, it was gone. All the way down. I feel so sick and weak. I can just imagine the disease that's starting in my poor stomach right now.'

'The flies are annoying,' Bonnie agreed, 'but I'm sure they have their place.'

'Not in my stomach,' Iris said crossly.

'No, of course not.' Bonnie battened down the urge to laugh with steely determination. 'Flies clean up refuse and even provide food for many other animals. And your stomach acid will make short work of any germs that went down with your fly if you did swallow it.'

She brought over the blood-pressure machine.

'But you look pale and I'd like to check your blood pressure. Are you sure you didn't hit your head when you fainted?'

'Hmph.' Still decidedly unimpressed, Iris shook her head. 'I don't want to see a nurse. I want to see a doctor.'

'That's harder. But certainly you can.' Bonnie smiled gently. 'But you'll have to go to Alice Springs for that. They have a very modern hospital there.'

'I think I will.' The little lady straightened her shoulders. 'How would I get there?'

Bonnie glanced at her watch. 'It's five hours by car but I've heard they've a scheduled bus that leaves from the mall.'

Iris swivelled her head and glared at Bonnie. 'What about an ambulance?'

Bonnie clamped down on her lips again. 'I'm afraid I'm the one who drives the ambulance and I have to be available here.'

The little lady visibly deflated and Bonnie wanted to pat her shoulder. Instead she soothed her. 'I swallowed a fly once and, apart from the thought, it didn't hurt me at all. I'm sure you'll be fine. But I'll check your blood pressure and get someone to help you back to your room so you can lie down until you feel better.'

Poor, unfortunate Iris nodded and sniffed and allowed Bonnie to fit the cuff and inflate it, but she wasn't happy.

When she'd finished, Bonnie patted Iris's arm. 'Your blood pressure's a bit low, so make sure you drink lots of fluids. It will go lower if you get dehydrated. Are you on any medications?'

'Won't take them.' Iris sighed. All of a sudden Iris seemed to shrink into the chair in front of her eyes and Bonnie felt her heart contract.

'I'm sorry.' Iris sniffed. 'I've been rude and un-grateful. I think I panicked a little.' She brushed her silver hair out of her eyes and sat up a little straighter. 'I used to be fearless you know, but after I lost my family, it seemed my nerves went at the same time.'

She sighed again. 'I always wanted to see the

Rock but it's not as much fun as I thought, on my own.' She rolled her shoulders and gathered her bag, then gingerly stood up.

Bonnie came around to stand next to her. She didn't know why she did it but she held open her arms and to her relief the little lady crept in for a brief hug. 'Iris, I believe you used to be fearless, you're still quite frightening when you want to be.' They smiled at each other. 'But I think you'll feel better soon.'

When she pulled back Iris smiled tremulously, and Bonnie could feel a little lump in her own throat. Iris needed companionship. Everyone did.

'I did hear the Sounds Of Silence Dinner is a wonderful place to meet fellow travellers,' Bonnie said. 'Please think about it for tonight. I promise you'll enjoy it. Even on your own.'

Bonnie followed Iris out into the waiting room and she was glad to see that, during the morning, between the efforts of Steve, Vicki and herself, all the chairs had finally become empty. 'Can you get someone to help Iris to her room for a lie-down, please, Vicki?'

'Of course.' She helped Iris to a waiting-room chair. 'And I'll make you a cup of tea while we wait.' She turned back to Bonnie. 'Can you see Steve, please, Sister? He has some news.'

When Bonnie entered the office Steve sat relaxed at the computer and sent a big grin Bonnie's way when she entered. 'We have a doc. He arrives this afternoon, the one I'd hoped for. Initially he cancelled but he's changed his mind.'

'That's great news.' Someone else to help with the ambulance, she thought thankfully. 'You know him?'

'He's a good friend, we grew up together, been out of circulation for a while. Lost his wife and child in a disastrous birth on his watch and he threw in the towel.'

Bonnie's palpitations hit her out of nowhere and her hand came up to her chest. She tried to keep her face from freezing and almost achieved it.

She licked her lips to ask the question but Steve went on.

'Harry was always great at getting to the root of a problem, mandatory around here when there's only us and disaster. Especially with our Aboriginal patients. Except with himself, I guess. He's been keeping to himself for a while now. But I think we're all like that when things go wrong.'

This could not be happening. 'That would be Harry St Clair?' Well, she'd told him to break out. She just hadn't planned on it being so soon and close. 'I thought he was in Bali.'

Steve glanced up. 'That's right. Inherited a house there. We'd been corresponding for weeks since the last guy dropped out. A friend met up with him for me a couple of days ago in a last-ditch attempt. Thought I'd lost. But he rang last night.' Steve grinned at her. 'So you know him too. That's great.'

'Great,' Bonnie echoed, and she wondered if her face was as white as it felt.

Now it wasn't just an event to try to forget. There'd be the constant reminder of how stupid she'd been. It was a full-blown disaster and she could kill him for doing this to her.

CHAPTER SEVEN

HARRY could feel the tension mount as the arid red landscape burned into his brain.

Memories of another flight, no premonition, the faces of those who waited for him, a tragedy that might never have happened if he'd ensured his wife had gone to the larger town when he'd said she should.

If he hadn't let himself be swayed by her wish to stay home a little longer.

Bonnie was right. He needed to face life and stop hiding from the past, though the pictures that clawed at him still scratched at his soul, though, just maybe, they seemed a little softer to him than before.

When they landed at Uluru Airport, the dry heat hit him like a hot newspaper in the face as he stepped off the plane, baked and arid—and he savoured the lack of humidity, so different from Bali.

It wasn't so bad being back—so far.

Steve waved from the gate and Harry lifted his hand in reply. Well, he'd have to perform now he was here. He'd hit the books since he'd booked his flight, hoping study would boost his confidence, maybe banish his ghosts, and he just had to trust it would all came back to him when that first obstetric crisis happened.

He really had no issues with emergency medicine—it was the babies and their mothers he didn't trust. No doubt Bonnie would be a whiz but he'd come to the conclusion she actually attracted maternal disasters, like a shiny lure on a fishing line.

He'd have none of that, thanks very much.

'So you made it.' Steve rubbed his hands together and Harry had to smile at his friend's enthusiasm.

'You don't have to baby me, Steve. I'll stay the month.'

Steve grabbed Harry's overnight case. 'Still got the old pack, I see. Vicki said hi. She's holding the fort with Bonnie.'

Harry kept his face impassive, he hoped, and it must have worked, because Steve went on, 'Our nurse. She said she's met you?'

Had he forgotten anything about her? He doubted it. 'Bonnie McKenzie. Tall, too thin, green eyes?'

'Don't know about the eyes…' Steve slanted him a glance '…but that's the one.'

Harry could see some serious questions and answers coming and tried diversion. 'So where's your car? I have to pick up the other box of stuff. I brought you some beer.'

'Cheers for that.' Steve rubbed his hands. 'Never enough beer in the desert. So when did you meet Bonnie?'

'Bali.' Nothing more. Hopefully they could leave it at that.

* * *

Bonnie was in the middle of suturing a trian-gular laceration on a young man's hand. She'd recognised the boy from the motorbike that first sunset.

'So, you came off your bike, Bernie?'

'Nah.' He grinned. 'Thumped a garbage bin 'cause my girlfriend got mad at me.'

Bonnie looked again and saw the way the scrape went from knuckle to knuckle and pic-tured it. Dumb kid. 'Make you feel better?'

A flash of white teeth in his ebony face. 'Yeah. Took me mind off me troubles.'

'What about the garbage bin?'

'Yeah. Came off better'n me.'

Bonnie shook her head. 'Men are strange.'

Harry walked in just as she said it. She glanced at him without a smile and tried to keep her face as neutral as possible. Not much else she could do. He looked disgustingly handsome and embar-rassingly familiar.

Steve followed him in, beaming. 'Bonnie, Harry's here. You two know each other.' Steve was happy. Obviously. He had his doctor and it was his friend as well. His world was good. 'I'm off to find Vicki to let her know we're back.'

Bonnie had no one but herself to blame for Harry deciding to come out of his shell in her direction. And she needed to remember it was a good thing for him to have made that choice. But he'd sucked her in once and she wasn't falling for his new pack of lies.

'Hello, Bonnie.' Harry smiled that killer smile and she fought to hide her body's instinctive reaction that, no matter what her brain said, decreed it was physically good to see him.

'Harry.' She nodded briefly and glanced at a point on the wall past his head. 'Australia not big enough for the two of us?'

'Seems not.' Out of the corner of her eye she could see he did look ridiculously glad to see her. Did he have short-term memory loss or something? They'd left a long way from being on best terms and she wasn't pretending they hadn't. Obviously she seriously didn't understand men so she looked back at Bernie's hand in front of her.

Unfortunately she could feel the warmth of just being in the same room as Harry seep into her like warm rays at sunrise creeping up a wall.

He stepped closer and peered down at her neat work. 'So you suture great as well,' he said.

She finished up the last stitch and tied it off. 'No one else to do it at some of the places I've been.' She peeled a dressing and sealed it into place. 'Try and keep it dry, Bernie. Come back in five days. I'll have another look and take the stitches out.' She winked at the boy and smiled. 'That okay with you?'

'Yep, missus.' Bernie picked up his cowboy hat and jammed it on his head. 'I'm gonna go see that girl of mine.'

'Just remember you have to look after her. She's feeling big and clumsy. Tell her she looks beautiful to you.'

Bernie grinned. ''Course she's beautiful.' He winked. 'And so are you.'

'Yeah, right.' Bonnie accepted that with a grain of salt. 'And take it easy on that bike of yours. I don't want to have to scrape you off the road.'

Bernie bolted out and Harry laughed. 'You've made a conquest.' He looked her up and down with serious warmth in his eyes. 'Another one.'

Bonnie washed her hands and dried them for longer than she probably needed to. Anything to hold off the moment when she had to look at him again. 'So what made you decide to take this job in the end?'

'Someone told me I should try medicine again. So I'm here to see what happens.'

She let him have an exaggerated sigh. She was tired of holding it back. 'I wasn't thinking about a place next to me.'

He raised his brows. 'You have a problem with me being here?'

'Yes would be the short answer.' Did she regret he was there? My word, she did. Even more so because he looked so darned good and her shoulders itched with memory of the weight of Harry's

arm around them. 'I might have made a few different decisions if I'd known we'd be working
together so soon.' Like backing off straight after
Jimbaran.

The silence lengthened while they both thought
about that until finally Harry stated the obvious.
'I'm only here four weeks.'

'I know. I've mentioned that to myself a couple
of times already today,' she said dryly. She steeled
herself and met his eyes. 'I won't trust you again,
Harry. You're not on a good wicket here.'

She wasn't sure what reaction she expected
from him but his sympathetic look made her eyes
prickle.

'Of course I understand that, Bonnie. What we
shared in Bali was based on my deceit, and I'm
sorry for that. Maybe one day you'll see how that
came about. But for now, what happened in Bali
is left in Bali. I got it.'

All very well to say that now. But the reasons
she'd given for allowing herself to sleep with
this man came back and bit her. There hadn't

been any good enough reasons. Even kissing and hand-holding would have made her skin heat with embarrassment. Let alone the fact that she knew every inch of his gorgeous body intimately.

This was ghastly.

So much for holiday flirtations not coming back to haunt you. She'd been such a fool and the heat still crept up her neck as she narrowed her eyes at him, trying to see if he meant it. She'd constantly underestimated his ability to con her. 'Okay.' Reluctantly her hand went out. 'Strictly platonic.'

'To platonicness.' Not a real word, so not a real vow, and a flippant comment that reminded her she was taking this more seriously than he was. What a surprise.

But when he took her fingers in his and gave them a quick shake, even with that fleeting contact, she knew anything to do with this man would have feelings and emotions attached to it.

Bonnie pulled away and turned her back. Damn. Damn and triple damn.

The rest of the day Harry spent with Steve and Vicki. Thankfully. It was good they worked out rosters, talked work, and despite Vicki's updates to Bonnie it seemed a lot of time was spent laughing over old times and Bonnie didn't feel excluded. Really. Honest.

By the end of the day Bonnie was drooping, exhausted, more from the nervous energy expended over coping with Harry's presence than the inconsistent workload. She could have done with a much busier workday to keep her mind occupied. Instead she'd been shoring up on her reasons not to fall under the spell Harry seemed to be able to weave over everyone. But not her. Certainly not her. She'd learnt her lesson.

There was a sticky moment when she remembered Harry's room was next door to hers but she didn't see him when she went to bed that night. He was still out with Steve and Vicki. By the time she'd reconciled herself to that it was after eleven and she was so exhausted she fell into a deep sleep when her head finally relaxed into the pillow.

When she woke in the morning, heavy-eyed and claustrophobic, she decided to return to the Rock for another dose of calmness.

Unfortunately when she pulled up Harry was just ahead of her and he saw her before she could turn around and drive away.

It was too late to avoid him now he'd stopped and was obviously waiting for her to catch up, and reluctantly she followed his footsteps in the red sand until she was standing beside him.

'Pleased I'm here, I see?' He didn't seem too perturbed and she wasn't in the mood to lie.

'No.'

He grinned at her. 'As soon as your plane left I missed your complimentary ways, you know that.'

'Don't tease me, Harry. My sense of humour is AWOL at the moment.'

'Okay. Let's enjoy the view.' He looked up at the monolith in front of them and raised his brows. The rock face above was in shadow still, and the darker areas seemed to have a life, a past life, and eons of stories to tell. 'Wow. Impressive.'

She glanced around and walked across until she could rest her hand on the granules of rock on the wall. She sighed. Cool and calm and having collected so much wisdom and experience. She could feel peace seep into her. 'Very.' He was right. She was there for healing, not for argument. And she guessed he was too. They did have to work together.

A peaceful walk sounded good. She buried her misgivings, tucked her hand in her jeans out of the way so she didn't swing her fingers into his, and set off.

A couple of hundred metres away, in the still coolness of the early morning, a toddler in a tracksuit wandered away from the visitor centre. She drifted further from her mum and her aunties and her grandmas cooking breakfast for the tourists to come, drifting across the sand like a floating grass seed, tiny footprints in the sand, a trail of flower imprints as she dawdled slowly, drawn towards the great monolith.

'Leila?' Her mother's voice also drifted towards the rock, and the little girl hesitated at the sound, but then a bird landed in front of her and she tottered after it.

When she came to the rock base a pool beckoned. The pool smiled at her and rippled with intriguing shifts of shadow and floating leaves and Leila reached down to capture a tiny twig that floated at the edge.

Bonnie and Harry nearly stumbled over the little girl as she peered into the grass beside one of the pools filled by last night's rain, and the memories of Bali slammed into both of them in the same instant. Not this time.

Bonnie's fingers reached down swiftly and gathered a handful of fabric from the little girl's jacket as a lifeline, and Harry was right beside her as they tried carefully not to startle the child or communicate the fear that had grabbed them both. Their eyes met. There was no way this poppet was falling in with them there.

Harry glanced around for the mother and suddenly in the still air she could hear a woman's frantic call. 'Leila?'

'Pretty,' said the little girl as she pointed to a lizard.

'Yes, it is pretty,' Bonnie said as she held out her hand. 'But you need to bring Mummy when you come here.' The little girl put her fingers in Bonnie's.

'Let's find Mummy, Leila.' Bonnie stood up and lifted the child into her arms as Harry cupped his hands over his mouth.

'She's here,' Harry called out. Their eyes met, and she knew they were both thinking of another little girl. She looked away as sudden tears stung her eyes at the memory of near tragedy. That was the only reason for the tears.

'She's fine,' Harry called out. 'On the path beside the base. With the nurse.'

Leila's mother burst from the bushes, her brow

beaded with perspiration and the stress of dread, and Bonnie passed the little girl into her arms.

'She was sitting beside the rock pool,' Harry said.

The mother looked at both of them with such relief in her face Bonnie felt tears sting her eyes again. She could only imagine a mother's fear.

'Thank you. I don't know how she got out but I'll work it out before tomorrow.' The woman clutched Leila to her chest. 'Don't do that, baby. You frightened Mumma.' The woman looked at Bonnie again. 'She slipped away while we made breakfast.'

Bonnie nodded. 'They're so quick, I know. She was watching the lizard over there, I think.'

'So close to the pool.' The mother shuddered. They all saw the lizard trundle off and Leila's mum smiled at the reptile as if it was a friend. 'That ngiyari can drink with his feet, you know. Water moves from his feet to his mouth along grooves in his skin. Very clever lizard. But my baby should not be here.' The mother squeezed her daughter and the little girl wriggled with de-light. 'Thank you, both. Again.'

Bonnie glanced up at the sky and guessed sun-rise would have taken place on the other side of the Rock by now. They'd have to go soon. 'I'm Bonnie, the new nurse and midwife at the clinic, and this is Dr St Clair. Maybe we'll meet again.'

'I'm Shay. We'll see you soon. My baby's due for her needles.'

Bonnie grinned. 'I'll be gentle.'

When the mother had gone Bonnie and Harry walked another fifteen minutes around the base and tried to regain the peace of the Rock but it was gone. Lost in the memory of another child who'd nearly drowned and the lies of the man beside her, all Bonnie could think of was the way Harry had almost left her to cope on her own. How he'd lied.

She didn't need this. She turned away and walked quickly back towards her car. He knew why.

The day was fairly quiet. A few cases of sunburn and a fractured cheekbone from a fall. And Leila's immunisations.

Bonnie smiled when she saw mother and daughter. It made her feel almost like she belonged here to see them again so soon.

'I thought I'd come while I remembered,' Shay said quietly. 'My aunty said bring her in today.' Bonnie managed to keep Leila diverted while she slipped the needle in and Shay was smiling by the time they left. 'Not as bad as I thought it would be,' she said. 'I'll tell my friends you're good with the little ones.'

By the end of the shift Bonnie was tired. Tired of knowing every minute of the day what Harry was doing, where he was standing, who he was talking to. And when he caught her eye and smiled it was even worse. That night it took her ages to fall asleep and when she did it didn't last long enough.

A call came through at midnight. Bonnie dreamt her phone was ringing, persistently, annoyingly, until she woke and found it really was.

The night concierge at Reception apologised quickly and then dropped his bombshell. 'We've a call from a guest that her husband had severe chest pain and now he's blue. Security will pick you and the doctor up in the ambulance to save time. He'll only be a minute or two away to take you there.'

Bonnie threw the bedclothes off. 'Of course. Is someone doing cardiac massage?'

'The night porter's there. He's trained in first aid. And the man's wife is doing the ventilation.' Amazing.

'Great work. I'll be ready.' Bonnie tore off her nightgown and dragged on her loose trousers and jumper. It was cold in the desert at night, though she had no doubt she'd be warming up with the adrenalin that was rushing through her body already. By the time she was hopping to the door, pulling on her shoes, she heard Harry's door open. She threw hers open just as he raised his hand to knock.

'Good,' he said, and she followed his disappearing back down the hallway and out to the ambulance that pulled up as they arrived.

It seemed he was no slouch when he decided to attend. At least she didn't have to worry about that. They scooted off into the night, and as the security man drove them along the twists and turns of the side roads between the bungalows she glanced at Harry's face.

Straight into a code one on his first night. He seemed calm and focused despite this being his first official emergency since he'd left medicine and the moment reminded her again of their last, much smaller patient—when he'd finally decided to help. She banished the thought and crossed her fingers for a similar positive outcome for the sick man and his family.

The bungalow door stood open and Harry jogged ahead while Bonnie grabbed the defibrillator. Bonnie could see the porter on his knees as he gave cardiac massage and the slight blonde woman with the big resuscitation bag between her elbows as she held the mask on her husband's face. She squeezed it twice after every thirty chest compressions.

The light from the ceiling shone off the perspiration on the porter's brow. Bonnie and Harry had come as soon as possible but five minutes must have felt like an hour for these poor people.

Harry slipped in beside the porter and took over the compressions.

'You're doing great. I'll take that from you in a moment,' Bonnie said to his wife, and knelt down and quickly undid the patient's pyjama jacket. Matted hair on the man's chest would confound the pad, she saw, and grabbed the razor to make two quick hairless areas to place the pads of the defibrillator. 'Darned hairy men,' Bonnie muttered under her breath.

When she had them attached in place she took the resuscitation bag from his wife, who collapsed back against the bed and watched as Harry ceased cardiac massage to view the tiny screen. Bonnie saw her jam her knuckles against her mouth and she nodded at her in sympathy. 'Hang in there.'

'Don't touch patient. Press shock button,' the recorded voice in the machine said in a monotone.

Harry said, 'All clear,' and glanced around to check before he pressed the shock button. The man's body lifted slightly off the floor and then sagged back.

Bonnie heard the man's wife gasp and glanced back over her shoulder with sympathy. 'He can't feel it. He's unconscious.'

Unconsciousness was the best scenario. They recommenced cardiac massage for another two minutes until the next ECG strip could be taken. The rhythm was slightly improved but not enough to sustain life. The message was repeated and they shocked him again. After the next two minutes of CPR the man began to shift and moan and Bonnie allowed a glimmer of hope to settle in her chest.

This time the screen showed a more viable rhythm and the man's colour began to improve.

Bonnie slid the oxygen mask onto the patient's face and put down the bag and mask, then handed Harry supplies for inserting an intravenous cannula on his side of the patient while she did the same on her side.

Within five minutes of their arrival the man was stable, even rousing to consciousness while being manoeuvred onto the stretcher of the ambulance in preparation for transfer to the medical centre.

Harry had already arranged on his mobile for the arrival of the Royal Flying Doctor Service to fly the man to Alice Springs. Pretty slick even for the most experienced of practitioners.

She glanced across at Harry as he gave another injection. There was no doubt they'd worked well together in this situation, though as far as Bonnie was concerned most of the thanks should really go to those first on the scene.

When Bonnie drove the ambulance to the medical centre, she found the cumbersome vehicle surprisingly easy to manoeuvre. Harry monitored the patient in the back, and the man's wife sat with her hands clasped together tightly in her lap in the front with Bonnie.

Bonnie finally had a moment to spare the woman some attention. 'Are you all right?' She glanced across at Clint's wife. 'Your husband's very lucky you knew what to do.'

Donna, their patient's ashen-faced wife, a petite fifty-year-old blonde, twisted her hands and swallowed the tears in her throat. 'Yes. Thank you.' She looked over into the back, bright tears running down her cheeks. 'Thank you both. All of you. The wonderful porter who took over from me. Those compressions.' She shuddered. 'I was so exhausted by the time he got there.'

'He looked a little weary too by the time we arrived, but you both did an incredible job of keeping the blood and oxygen circulating.'

Donna ran her hand over her face to wipe away the tears. 'I never want to have to do that again.

Thank goodness you came. Those portable de-fibrillators are incredible, aren't they?'

Bonnie could see Donna needed to talk. Needed to dump some of the nervous energy she'd been holding back so incredibly. She'd been amazing. What a heroine. 'They're very handy. And so quick to do the job.'

She thought of Donna's husband's hairy chest and smiled. 'I'm afraid Clint's going to have two shaved areas on his chest. Like two big eyes. Not very neat either.'

'He'll cope. I might wax the lot of him while he's unconscious,' Donna shakily joked, 'ready for next time.'

Bonnie took her hand off the wheel and patted Donna's shoulder. 'Hopefully he'll be sorted out by his doctor and there won't be a next time. But I think you're incredible, the way you're holding yourself together.'

Bonnie saw more tears spring into Donna's eyes. Oops, sometimes sympathy wasn't help-ful. She should have known that. Bonnie hastily changed the subject. 'The medical system here is very efficient. All the mod cons as well.' Bonnie pulled into the medical centre.

The next few minutes were taken up by transferring the patient to a ward bed and connecting him to the wall monitors. When they had Clint settled Bonnie went back to Donna, who'd been in contact with their grown-up children on the phone.

'The children are so appreciative. And impressed,' Donna said. 'I think he had more chance here than if he'd had the heart attack at home in Sydney.'

Bonnie smiled. 'You might be right. But a lot of the outcome depends on what other people do in those crucial first few minutes. You called for help and got on with it. You did everything right.' She smiled. 'I think you're marvellous. So it couldn't have been his time to go.'

'My word, it's not.' Donna glanced across at her husband as if to check he was still there. 'We've worked hard all our lives and he's not losing his retirement because of ill health. I'll make sure he eats the right things and does an exercise programme. In fact, I'll do it with him.'

Harry joined them. 'Sounds great. We all need to.'

Bonnie gestured with her hand. 'Harry. Dr St Clair. This is Donna, Clint's wife.'

'Hello, Donna. We didn't have much time to chat, did we? The night porter said you were terrific with the CPR before he arrived.'

'Thank you, Doctor. I hope I never have to do that again but as I said to Bonnie, I'm not losing him now. We've got too much fun to have yet. Too many children together and too much history.' Donna's voice shook on the last word.

Bonnie felt tears sting her own eyes. History. Would she ever have that kind of history with a man in her life? Not just bad memories and brief emotional flings with liars and losers?

She saw the way Harry closed down, too. As if he didn't want to know about history, and children and wives losing husbands, or vice versa.

Maybe she would understand more if she knew the circumstances of his loss but she refused to ask Steve or Vicki. It was Harry's story and if he didn't think she needed to know, she'd be fine with that. Either way, it wasn't her business. She'd keep it that way.

By the time Clint was flown out it was almost dawn. Harry and Bonnie saw Donna back to her room, which Housekeeping had tidied for her, and Bonnie tucked her in.

Harry waited at the door. 'Have a couple of hours' sleep, and Reception will help you get an early flight. It will truly take that long to get him settled into the ward and the tests will take up most of the morning until you get there. Try not worry too much.'

As they walked away, Harry captured Bonnie's hand and held it. 'Well done, Bonnie.'

She was not going there! Bonnie eased her hand free and kept her voice level. 'You should say, "Well done, team."'

'Actually...' Now that she thought about it, she

stopped walking until he stopped too. 'Imagine if you hadn't decided to come and that was all on me and the porter?'

He frowned as if to say, 'So?'

She shook her head at his refusal to understand. 'This is exactly what I meant at the airport at Denpasar. I can't give some of those drugs, Harry. Not without medical orders. That all takes time and I really don't think Clint had time.'

She saw his comprehension settle. 'Maybe,' he said, still reluctant but aware of what she was getting at. Finally he nodded. 'Yes. I'm glad I was here for that. And for Clint.' He looked at her. 'And for you. I don't like to think of you having to cope with emergencies like that on your own, Bonnie.'

'People have to if the resources aren't there. Like you did before you gave up medicine.'

He frowned. They arrived back at the Desert Pea and Harry held the door for her. He didn't comment on her words.

And he wouldn't. Why should she be surprised? Bonnie yawned. 'Shame about a night's sleep.'

Harry glanced at the lightening sky. 'You go to bed. Stay there till lunchtime if you can. I won't sleep. I'll ring you if I need you. Maybe you can relieve me this afternoon when I crash.'

She glanced at him and she could tell he was wired. He wasn't shutting his eyes any time soon. She guessed he did have a lot to think about. And she was stuffed. 'Sounds very democratic. Goodnight.'

Harry watched her close her door and for a brief moment wished he could just follow her into her room and never come out, but he turned away. He'd burned his boats there. Best go for a walk around the grounds, let the morning air wash away the tension, and when he got back he could ring Alice Springs and see if Clint had arrived safely.

Harry flexed his shoulders. So he was a little unsettled by the last few hours but he was beginning to accept he just might be in the right place for him at this time. At least he wasn't dreading that first day on call any more.

Later that morning, Harry discovered he might not have offered to do the clinic if he'd realised it was antenatal clinic day. It was all very well to begin to feel more comfortable with medicine, but pregnant women were way too close to home.

By the time Bonnie surfaced about eleven he'd recovered his equilibrium, but his face lit up when she arrived. 'You could take over here, Bonnie.'

Bonnie smiled when she saw who the clients were. 'Hi, guys.'

Bernie's pearly white grin lit up the room and he nudged his girlfriend. 'She's the nurse I said about.'

Harry smiled at Bernie's delight. 'I was just saying to Tameeka that she should think about how long she stays in Alice Springs as she approaches her due date. In fact, she's only got five weeks to go she may as well go soon.'

Bonnie saw the frowns on both young people's faces and glanced between the three of them, feeling her way to diplomacy. 'Women usually wait until two weeks before their due date if they move into town.'

That didn't go down well with the medical officer. 'I disagree.' Harry shook his head to underline it. 'We have no idea when that first baby is going to arrive and this isn't a safe place to have baby without the hospital.'

Bonnie tried not to telegraph her feelings but it was a battle she only just won. She wanted to frown like her patients were at this insensitive goose.

She tried another angle, hoping that Harry would get the hint. 'Do you have anyone you can stay with, Tameeka?'

Unhappily, the girl shook her head and rolled her eyes at Bernie. Bernie spoke for her. 'She's worried about bein' homesick 'cause I can't stay up there. I gotta job down here with the traditional owner tours. I work mornings from five till eleven. She don't need to go yet. It's only a five-hour drive.'

Bonnie lifted her brows and tried to lighten the mood of the conversation. 'Might be interesting, having contractions on a motorbike.'

'Nah.' Bernie grinned. 'My cuz has a car and he'll take us when she goes into labour.'

Harry shook his head. 'You can't wait until she's in labour.' He turned to Bonnie and mouthed, 'Talk some sense into them, please.' Out loud, he said. 'We'll see what we can arrange.' And left Bonnie to it.

'What's up his jumper?' Bernie said as Harry walked away.

'Apart from being up all night at an emergency, he wants what's best for Tameeka and your baby, that's all.' Inside, Bonnie was fuming. What a lot of angst for nothing.

If they sent Tameeka too early she'd get home-sick and come home again anyway. Then they'd have a devil of a time getting her back to Alice Springs for the actual birth. Bonnie dealt with these issues all the time on outreach clinics. Heavy-handed tactics weren't helpful at all.

Didn't he realise it was a terrifying thing for the young woman to be sent to a large town on her own to give birth? Well, Bonnie would do what was necessary to smooth that path and hopefully it wouldn't all backfire in her face. Life might have more facets of frustration with Harry than she'd anticipated.

Harry walked away and he could feel the rigid set of his shoulders as he fought panic.

Everything had been going along fine until he'd realised Tameeka was exactly the same length of time into her pregnancy as his wife had been when she'd died. Thirty-five weeks.

That awful paralysing fear had grabbed him by the throat and he'd wanted to put the young woman on a plane and get her to safety. Get her off his hands. Away from his responsibility. Let Alice Springs deal with her birth and she and her baby could come home well.

Which was ridiculous. Tameeka might not go

into labour for another four weeks. Bonnie was right. But he also knew a person who feared the natural process of birth should not be caring for pregnant women. And that included him.

Needless interventions, like sending pregnant women away too early, didn't help anyone. The inherent dangers if she came back and refused to leave again, increased risk of car accidents from multiple trips and postnatal depression from a lonely stint away from her family all had to be weighed up.

He didn't know what the answer was. Except now he was wishing he hadn't come.

CHAPTER EIGHT

AT THE end of the first week, Bonnie waited for the Sounds of Silence Dinner bus in the reception area with all the tourists. She doubted she'd have arranged it so soon except that when Clint had been flown out by the RFDS, Donna had given Harry and herself the tickets they couldn't use. And the porter loved the bottle of Scotch that Donna had said Clint wasn't going to open now.

It felt odd to be dressed up to eat on a sand dune but Vicki and Steve had been adamant it added to the ambiance of the evening. Even odder when she reminded herself who her dinner companion was.

When Harry arrived in dark trousers and a white shirt stark against his tan, the other women waiting swivelled to admire him, and Bonnie smiled wryly as she watched them compare the two of them. Just like in Bali.

'You look gorgeous,' Harry said, and the way his eyes lingered reminded her how accomplished he was at beaming light at her. She remembered how she'd thought of him as a lighthouse the first time she'd seen him.

Funny how she forgot about the competition in an instant and even forgot how well she knew this man. Actually, she forgot about everything except the powerful way he could draw her in like a merman to his shipwrecking rocks. Watch those rocks, she told herself.

That day he'd come over to talk to her at the swimming pool seemed so long ago and such a convoluted dance they'd been in since then. So much for not being one of his harem of admirers.

At least he didn't turn it on at work.

Or maybe she had a force field when she was with a patient because after that first day or two she could separate the two then, helped immeasurably by that not-so-little issue of trust that she didn't have with him now.

But tonight she could feel herself weaken. Pathetic woman. 'Well, thank you, you're looking debonair yourself.'

Harry's fingers rested on her elbow as he steered her out to the arriving bus and the warmth of his possession ran up her arm. It was happening again. Waves of awareness tingling in her skin, heat, low and hard in her belly. Lordy, yes, this man made her know she was alive.

He leant down and spoke into her ear so the others couldn't hear. 'What's the chance you get through this night without a call out?'

It was hard to listen when she was feeling so intensely. It felt so good to be hip to hip again. Too good to have his hand on her skin and his face near hers.

She pulled back, needing to make a play for some distance. 'Fair to poor. But I'm going to enjoy the moments I do get. My friend in Darwin has been talking about this dinner since she did a stint here.' Now she was babbling. There had to be a happy medium.

He ushered her up the steps of the bus and into a window seat. His hip was against hers as the bus took off on the ride out to the dunes, the excited chatter of their dinner companions a hum around them.

Bonnie felt Harry's leg near hers, like on the bus on the day of the bike ride, but she was pretty sure she wasn't going to end up naked in his arms like she had that day. She blushed. She had better not. It would be a lot harder to hide the damage from a repeat performance of gullibility.

She looked desperately out the window towards the orange and red hues of near sunset. There was the Rock, she thought with relief, and hung on to that magnificent vision like a lifejacket.

Bonnie breathed in the sheer magic like an antidote. Slowly she gained a measure of stability. The sight filled her head until she could shift aside Harry for a moment and the issues they had, and just savour Mother Earth at her most majestic.

'Gorgeous,' she said as she turned back to Harry and found him watching her, studying her profile as if he couldn't understand something, and she felt her neck heat as she resisted the urge to give in and blush.

'Have I got a smut on my nose or something?'

He laughed without humour. 'Not that I can see.'

Bonnie frowned at him. They couldn't do this. Work together and continue the level of awareness they generated between them. She opened her mouth to broach the idea of strategies for managing that when she reminded herself they were surrounded by other people.

Funny how the world seemed to narrow down to just the two of them when she was with Harry.

In the end it didn't matter because the bus jerked to a halt, out in the middle of the desert between the two great icons of central Australia, the single massive of Uluru and Kata Tjuga, the huge collection of enormous boulders that made up the Olgas.

As she stepped off the bus Bonnie didn't know which way to turn, to watch the sun reflected against the rock or setting behind the Olgas, and the choice was an awe-inspiring dilemma.

Harry gestured to the silk rope and suggested she follow the guests up the incline to the top of the dune where a tuxedoed waiter stood with silver tray of champagne in crystal glasses.

The setting was beyond anything she'd expected. 'Thank you,' Bonnie said, and took a half-full glass from the man and slowly turned to admire the full view from the top of the dune. She crossed to the bar and at her request the waiter filled her glass with soda water. Harry did the same and she smiled at him. 'Trying to get into my good graces?'

'Not fair for just you to be on call.' She'd never said he wasn't thoughtful but she'd prefer if he made it easier to keep her distance and not harder.

They turned back to face the Rock. Neither spoke as the chiselled face of the massif grew more shadowed with wrinkled stone and signs of weathering in gold and different pinks that seemed to glow brighter. Too beautiful. As a backdrop, the dark velvet red of the desert, with sparse desert oaks interspersed up and down the rolling mini-dunes, blushed with its own radiance.

'Kangaroo, crocodile or Tasmanian salmon.' The waitress offered tiny hors d'oeuvres with cress on crackers, and Bonnie blinked as the spell was broken.

She glanced at Harry, suddenly more composed. She did feel better. More grounded and relaxed with him. She could do this without making a fool of herself.

The idea of eating a wallaby wrinkled her nose, but crocodiles often ate humans so it seemed fair to return the favour. 'Thank you.' She glanced at Harry, darkly handsome as he watched her, and she pretended she wasn't perturbed by his study. Hers was a front but a fairly good one.

'After luwak coffee I'll try anything.' Bonnie took a serviette and biscuit with crocodile meat and nibbled at the edge of it. See, she could even allude to a previous time. She was strong. It was quite an act not to drop crumbs or her lass but her composure held.

Her juggling must have looked a little dangerous because Harry collected another serviette for her with a smile.

'Maybe we should take turns, and the other person can hold the glass, like an old married couple.'

Harry using the *M* word. Good grief. And he didn't look happy about it. She glanced away. 'There's a few of those here. Lucky things, to be travelling round together. Clint and Donna should be here. They'd fit right in.'

He didn't quite wrinkle his nose but he turned his shoulder to block out the concept of happily married couples. 'Let's move to a spot with a bench so we can sit and just relax to enjoy the view.'

Harry's aversion to marriage and happy couples was getting a bit old actually. Bonnie had no problem enjoying the history of the other couple. They found a spot on a rustically weathered log and as Bonnie emptied her hands she spotted Iris, her silver-haired, fly-swallowing lady from the first day, and waved.

Harry lifted one eyebrow as Iris bustled across, all chiffon and pearls, dragging a twinkle-eyed gentleman, and when she arrived she even kissed Bonnie's cheek.

'Hello, there, dear.' Iris was glowing. 'How lovely to see you.' She glanced over her shoulder at her beau. 'Fergus is a widower. We met last night. We had such a wonderful time that Fergus asked me to come with him again tonight.'

Bonnie shook the man's hand. 'That's lovely, Iris. Hello, Fergus. This is Harry, the doctor I work with.'

'Harry.' Fergus smiled and they shook hands

too. Bonnie pointed to the tray as it went past held by a smiling waitress.

'Have you tried the crocodile?'

Iris giggled. 'I said to Fergus, if I can eat a fly I can eat a crocodile.' She glanced affectionately up at the elderly gentleman who looked down at her with an amused air. 'He thinks I'm silly.'

'Och, that's no' true. I think you're a sweet wee gasbag and a lot of fun. Now, let's leave these young ones to enjoy their evening while I whisper sweet nothings in your ear.'

Iris waved and Bonnie couldn't help the grin on her face as she watched them walk away. 'That's great. A gorgeous Scotsman. She was so sad when I met her earlier in the week.'

'You're a softy. Care about each person, don't you?' Harry said. 'Really wish them well. Anyone and everyone.' He shook his head at the concept, pretended he didn't subscribe to it too. 'Not everyone is like that.'

She drained her glass. 'I know for a fact you care, so don't give me that. I've seen you in action in Bali. The kids on the bikes, that first night we met. Even the people here.' She stared at him. 'It's what we do, Harry. Why we do it. Coming back to medicine might help you find the large part of you that's missing.' She felt the wall go up.

'So I'm guessing you like it here.' Harry changed the subject and she mentally shrugged. It was still like being in a minefield, talking to him.

'I'm enjoying myself. I'd like more midwifery, but apart from the antenatal visits for the women from the settlement, as you've already said quite strongly, labours need to be shipped out. So I won't see much of that. But I'm enjoying the diversity.'

'Steve and Vicki do a good job.' They took two more hors d'oeuvres as they went past and conversation gave way to pleasure in the view.

She nodded and sighed happily over the sunset that grew more spectacular by the second, and without looking at him tried for some history that wouldn't upset him. 'So, tell me how you know Steve?'

He put his glass down. 'We grew up together, in Darwin. Went to the same schools, same group of friends, got married in the same year.'

He'd even mentioned his wife. That was a first. 'So your wife was from Darwin too?'

'No.' He stood up and looked at the bar. 'Do you want a soft drink? I think I'll get one.' Slam. End of conversation.

'Sure.' She stood up herself. 'I might go and chase the waitress for another one of those crocodile biscuits.'

Bonnie circulated among the other guests, Iris introduced her around, she spoke to the wait staff she'd seen in the Desert Pea accommodation and avoided looking for Harry.

When they were called through the silk rope again from the top of the dune down to where the tables were laid out in the desert below, he appeared beside her in time to be her dinner companion, along with six other people at their circular table.

She wasn't sure she'd have been so efficient. 'I thought you might have preferred to sit next to someone less nosy.'

He touched his own nose. 'You're not nosy. I'm just out of practice answering to anyone.'

'That's your right. Sorry if I upset you, Harry.' She chose her seat and tucked her bag under her chair.

He waited until she was seated, then sat down and they shared the sight of the vastness of the Olgas in front of them across the stretching desert. 'You haven't a mean bone in your body, Bonnie. Let's just enjoy the night.'

Bonnie chose to admire the snowy cloth and the silver cutlery and the glasses that shone in the candlelight. Much better than feeling patronised, and a little irritated, even isolated below the stars that slowly appeared out of the darkening night sky, which was ridiculous. Other people introduced themselves, so there were other people apart from Harry here, she must remember that. This was getting old too.

She joined in the introductions that followed, appreciated the revelry as the champagne the others were drinking, even if she wasn't, relaxed her dinner companions and loosened their tongues. It seemed they had a party of couples towing their caravans around Australia at their table.

'Been on the road for three months,' one of the husbands said with a grin, and his wife rolled her eyes. One of the other women giggled.

'We're in our fifth month,' another commented, and Bonnie listened in awe as they spoke of the places they'd seen and the unexpected adventures they'd found. She couldn't imagine being with one person for months on end in a vehicle. She certainly couldn't imagine Harry doing it, but by the end of a long dinner and their companions, at least, draining the replenished red and white wine, she could see the fun of it.

Later that night, when the bus dropped them

off, even Harry found himself returning to the staff quarters more relaxed than he'd expected.

He heard Bonnie say, 'I had a ball.'

And it was actually easy to say, 'Me too.'

He could see Bonnie still smiling over the risqué comments that had followed them off the bus and suddenly he didn't want the night to end. Didn't want to lose the connection they'd built up over the evening. A connection he hadn't felt since Ubud, which, of course was his own fault.

'Fancy a pot of tea? Don't know about you but the evening seemed to end a bit suddenly for me.'

'Sounds good.' Bonnie looked up into the sky, searching for newly identified constellations, not so easy to see with all the lights around them. Out in the desert they'd extinguished the lights, the darkness had opened the whole sky to them, and it was a sight she'd never forget.

She spun around as she tried to identify the stars. 'It was much easier when the astronomer pointed them out.'

She sounded plaintive, and Harry smiled to

himself. Her eyes had been brighter than any of the stars they'd seen tonight. She'd been so excited to learn the names of the constellations and individual celestial bodies when the stargazer had told stories and myths from the past. He remembered how she'd been interested in the stars that night at Jimbaran.

'Come inside before Security decides you're up to no good.'

Bonnie turned her head and waved at the man with his torch who was circling the building. 'I reckon he'd recognise us from the other night, but okay.'

They slipped in the front door and headed for the recreation room. 'You make the tea, I'll grab a box of chocolates from my room.' Bonnie was gone before he could answer.

Harry turned the lights on in the communal dining room and plugged in the jug. Maybe this wasn't such a good idea. Every moment he spent with Bonnie made it harder not to pull her into his arms and find that peace he knew was there.

The feeling of rightness he hadn't lost since the magic of Ubud.

It had been like that with Clara too, he reminded himself. He didn't even want to think about the differences between Clara and Bonnie. He had enough guilt.

There'd been magic with Clara too, and then before he'd known it he had been set up for heartbreak and disaster. No way was he going back. He had the horrors even imagining Bonnie in danger. And it wasn't fair for him to not make that fact plain to Bonnie. Tonight.

On her side she'd kept the relaxed rapport from the evening. He could see that when she arrived back clutching an unopened box of chocolates. 'My friends in Darwin gave me these. I'll never eat them on my own. Seems right for tonight.'

She ripped open the box. Delightfully exuberant. 'I had a great time.' Bonnie popped a white sweet into her mouth and sighed blissfully. She sank back into the chair with her eyes closed.

He reached across and chose a dark nutty one

with a twisted curl on top. Serious decision-making while he edged his brain around how he was going to say this. 'Me too. Considering my behaviour earlier.'

She shrugged that away. 'You didn't want to talk about it.'

But he did now. 'I want to apologise, though.'

She didn't open her eyes. 'Okay. Done. Let's talk about something else.'

He supposed it was her turn to avoid unpleas-antness but he needed Bonnie to understand how drawn he was to her, keen to spend time together if she was interested, but no strings and no future.

Not that she'd asked for any, and maybe the clarification was more for him than her, but he needed to say it. That he wasn't opening himself for that kind of pain again.

The jug boiled and he got up and poured the water in the pot and put the cups on the table. Neither of them took milk. He'd learned that at least since he'd arrived. He sat down. 'I'm guessing you haven't asked Steve what happened to my wife and I. I appreciate that.'

Bonnie sat up and pointedly stared down at the chocolate choice in the box. He wished she'd look at him so he could see what she was thinking. Her posture suggested she didn't want to hear and he was sorry about that.

After the relaxed evening it was probably a downer but she'd been happy to blast him at the airport and the sting lingered. She'd hear it and then they could both get on with their own lives.

She sighed and when she did look his way her eyes were the windows to the soul he'd expected. She'd accepted the conversation wasn't going to go away.

'Okay,' she said quietly. 'So you didn't meet your wife in Darwin.' She remembered his earlier statement. Of course she did. He'd bet she remembered a lot of things—some he wasn't proud of.

'I met Clara in Alice Springs. She did her training there and I met her again in Katherine when I started working for the RFDS.'

Bonnie so didn't want to do this now. 'Small planes make me sick. I could never nurse and fly at the same time.' It had been a pleasant evening, she'd been proud of herself as she'd made headway with her plans of distancing Harry by being friendly and concentrating on other people. Drinking tea late at night was not good for distance. She should have stayed in her room.

She'd begun to feel queasy just knowing he was going to talk about his loss.

Did he have to ruin a great night? Did she really need to understand him? She was beginning to think the less she knew of Harry St Clair the better for her own sake, but she doubted she had a choice now he'd started.

Harry poured both teas. 'I never felt sick, flying. Usually too busy with a patient to think about my stomach.' His response came out lightly but she could see his mind was elsewhere.

Okay. Stop beating around the bush. Do it.

Bonnie just wanted this over with. 'So how long were you married?' *How long before she died?* she really wanted to ask.

'A year. But probably came down to a few months by the time you took out the amount of time I was away. We should never have got married, or at least I wasn't keen on it until I had a less mobile job, but we did and very soon she fell pregnant, though we weren't planning on that either.'

This was it. The reason he was how he was. Her voice dropped. 'So what happened, Harry?'

'Amniotic fluid embolism. Early labour.'

Bonnie felt her heart sink. Not nice at all.

'We were in an outlying area. She should have gone to town at thirty-six weeks, been closer to the hospital. I wasn't even there till near the end. Didn't know what was happening. Nobody guessed. Everything should have been fine. No risk factors.'

Ouch. So he had no faith in natural labour. 'Rare and horrible,' Bonnie said quietly. 'We've had one in Darwin, though before my time, and I think I read that the incidence as one in about twenty-six thousand. You can't predict that. And not great odds if they do diagnose it when it happens.'

'Yeah. Usual diagnoses made at autopsy.' He grimaced. 'Clara was a previously healthy woman, healthy pregnancy, but they found her uterus had a small rupture during early labour, must have been congenital, and the amniotic fluid got into her bloodstream, caused an allergic reaction. She collapsed and even though we did an emergency caesarean we couldn't save her. I couldn't save her. Couldn't save my baby, though we tried. That resus nearly killed me. Certainly killed any desire to go back to medicine.'

'Until now.'

He lifted his head and his eyes narrowed. 'Who's fault is that?'

She wasn't taking the blame. No way. 'Not mine. Nobody forced you. You're your own man.

But I'm glad you did. And I'm pretty sure Clint and Donna are too.'

His mind was still on Katherine with his own tragedy. No wonder she felt there was a part of him missing half the time. 'I don't know what I'd do if I came across it again.'

'Are you sure of that?' Bonnie didn't agree. 'Maybe you'd use what you learnt last time, pick it up way before anyone else, and give mother and child the chance they might not have had with the insight you gained. So that your wife and child's lives weren't wasted.'

He turned tortured eyes on her and Bonnie felt the squeeze in her heart that she was kidding herself if she thought she could stay immune to the hurt this man suffered. She was already too involved.

'It's the picture, Bonnie.' The words were barely a whisper. 'Her face as white as the hospital sheet.' He shook his head. 'My baby growing cold. It's engraved on my soul.'

Bonnie felt her own heart rip. She stood up,

moved to his chair and crouched down to put her arm around him. She rested her cheek against his.

'It's incredibly sad. And so hard on you. But maybe you should try to see there's another side of the picture, Harry. Imagine it, because I can. It happened a minute or so later. Clara blowing you a kiss as she floated out the window, to heaven, with her baby. The two of them together, Harry, hand in hand. Sending you love for your pain but themselves at peace. Not bothered by pain or regret or fear.' She leaned over and kissed his mouth. Willing his pain to ease. 'There was nothing you could do.' Quietly and firmly she said the words he must have heard a hundred times before. Maybe this time he could allow himself to believe.

She believed it. It was the kind of image her gran had given her when her mum and dad had died, and the relief had been enormous. And healing. She wanted to share that with this man who'd inched his way into her heart, when a man in her heart was the last thing she wanted.

It was all in his face when he looked at her. Really stared her down while he thought about it, and she wondered if she'd gone too far. His face stayed unreadable, a pain-filled mask she couldn't see through, the huge wall between them bigger than it had ever been, like the Rock outside her window, but she couldn't take it back. Because she believed it true with all her heart.

Then he stood up and just walked away. Left her sitting there, staring after him, wondering, hoping, wishing she'd kept her mouth shut.

The next morning Bonnie woke early and lay in bed and watched the stars fade outside her window. Her head still spun from Harry's disclosures the night before and the picture of tragic disaster he'd painted.

It was a good premonition for what was to come.

CHAPTER NINE

TAMEEKA'S auntie wore a bright red football jumper and orange shorts. A big, rangy woman, she had square, bare feet still dusty from the road and she ushered the sheepish teens into the medical centre with an expansive wave of her hand.

It was late afternoon and Bonnie observed the young pregnant woman's apprehensive face and looked around for Harry. He was going to blow his top.

Her mind darted for answers as she waved them in. They could get the RFDS aircraft in if the plane wasn't half a world away, helping someone else, or they could take the ambulance and meet the Alice Springs ambulance two and a half hours up the road.

But getting to a hospital in time was the question. Damn not having a midwifery facility here.

She shook off her wishes and put them aside. 'Hello, there, you must be Tameeka's Auntie Dell. She said you'd be with her. I'm Bonnie.' She smiled at Tameeka and a nervous Bernie. 'Come through, honey. What happened to Bernie's cousin's car?'

Bernie shrugged. 'He went on walkabout two days ago and he's not back yet.'

Bonnie glanced at the clock on the wall. 'So what time did the pains start, Tameeka?'

'Not long ago.' The young girl wouldn't meet Bonnie's eyes, which wasn't that unusual, but Bonnie had her suspicions when the next contraction rolled around very firmly within the minute and lasted a good sixty seconds.

'I told her she 'ad to come.' Auntie Dell was born to be an authority figure and probably had a dozen nieces she'd be shepherding into labour. 'You're that nurse who picked up little Leila, aren't you?'

'Yes. Are you Shay's auntie too?' Bonnie smiled. She turned back to help Tameeka sit down. 'Thanks for bringing her in.'

It was a shame Tameeka hadn't seen her aunt a little earlier, Bonnie thought ruefully. That would have been good. But it didn't really matter when her labour had started. The past was the past, and it was what happened now that counted.

She had the sudden notion that concept should apply to Harry too, but she'd hear enough from him in a minute without pre-empting him.

'It's all good. You're here now. Do you mind if I have a feel of your tummy and listen to that gorgeous baby of yours, please, Tameeka?'

Tameeka lay down on the examination couch and Bonnie met her eyes before she attempted to feel. 'Okay if I feel the way baby is lying?' Tameeka nodded and Bonnie gently palpated the mound of ebony skin as she felt for the baby's back, bottom and head. She smiled. 'Your baby seems to know the way out. He or she's pointing the right way.'

Bonnie placed the nozzle of the little handheld foetal heart monitor on Tameeka's stomach and the sound of a baby's heartbeat filled the air.

'Love the sound of them babies.' Auntie Dell smiled beatifically. Bonnie nodded in agreement as she counted the beats.

'What if it's too late to go?' Bernie asked the question but it was there too, in Tameeka's eyes as plain as day.

Auntie Dell huffed, 'You'd be in trouble, bro.'

Bonnie softened the rebuke. 'Babies decide when and where they come. But we might get Tameeka to Alice Springs in time yet. At least she won't be sitting there by herself, waiting. It looks like it's going to happen today and I'm sure Bernie can miss one day off work.'

'Too right. I'm not leaving her.'

'I'm not leavin' either.' Auntie Dell planted her hands on her hips. Bonnie smiled to herself. She wasn't going to take on forcing Auntie Dell to stay behind so it was going to be tight in the ambulance if they had to drive.

'Who's not leaving?' Harry arrived with a measured tread and Bonnie's antenna picked up the underlying pressure in his voice. At least the face he showed the young couple was non-judgemental and she allowed herself to relax a little. Of course he'd be fine. Except Tameeka was in labour a long way from a hospital.

Tameeka's abdomen grew tight and she rolled her eyes as another strong contraction informed everyone it meant business.

'How long's this been going on?' Now Harry's eyes held a tiny hint of accusation when he looked at Bonnie. He'd have loved to blame her, she could see that. She guessed it helped to blame someone and she was the logical choice. Men!

'Not long. They've just arrived.' Bonnie's calmness eased the tension that had begun to tighten the room and Harry looked at the young couple.

Bonnie could almost see Harry's mind sorting options. He shot a look at Bonnie. 'Have you examined her yet?'

'Just felt her tummy. Head down, well engaged.'

He nodded. 'Tameeka, I'd like Bonnie to feel how far along in your labour you are. We have to tell the Flying Doctors when we ring them. Is that okay?'

Tameeka nodded and Bernie gulped and eyed the door. Bonnie could see he'd decided to leave this bit of women's business to the women and followed Harry out.

Bonnie heard him mutter to Harry as they shut the door. 'She said them pains didn't hurt too much and I thought it was them Baxtin Icks, practice pain things.'

The three women smiled at each other at the thought processes of men as Tameeka slipped her underwear off.

Bonnie folded the sheet back from the bottom of the bed. Tameeka closed her eyes and nodded for Bonnie to go ahead.

Bonnie pulled on her gloves and stared at the wall opposite as she concentrated on what she could feel. 'Okay. I can touch your baby's head a little way inside but not too far. The bottom of your uterus is very thin, pointing to the front, and opened enough for two finger widths. So that's nearly three centimetres dilated. The baby has his or her chin well tucked in so that's good.'

Bonnie stood back and removed her gloves. 'Your baby's head is right down so when you get a contraction it leans on the opening and makes the cervix a little bit wider each time. That's why the more regular the contractions, the quicker your labour.'

'What about them waters?' Auntie Dell had her hands on her hips again.

Bonnie turned back. She was getting to that but she had an idea Tameeka had a little more trouble following what she was talking about than Auntie Dell. She smiled at the older lady. 'The bag of waters is still there and Tameeka will probably still have a few hours of labour before her baby is born. Maybe enough to get to Alice Springs.'

Bonnie listened again briefly with the foetal heart Doppler to check the baby didn't mind somebody touching his or her head and then stepped back to wash her hands.

When she came back to the bed Auntie Dell had helped Tameeka up and to dress again. Bonnie looked at both of them. 'Any questions?'

'Can I stay here and have my baby with my auntie?'

Bonnie would have loved that but it wasn't an option they had with no backup. 'Unfortunately not. But we can try really hard to keep your auntie and Bernie with you until you have your baby.'

In the end, despite Harry's phone calls, the RFDS were away in Kakadu and Harry decided they'd use the road ambulance. He wasn't keen on the presence of Auntie Dell and refused to see the problem.

'There's not much room in an ambulance and she's a big lady.' It seemed he wanted to be obtuse today and Bonnie was fast losing patience. 'I don't see how she can come,' he said.

They were outside the room and talking in low voices as they waited for Steve to bring the ambulance round. Bonnie almost laughed out loud. Fat chance of Auntie Dell staying behind.

'I'm interested, Harry. What do you need room for? Tameeka's a healthy woman, early in active labour, doing what she's designed to do. If you're sure we can't have her baby here, with the option of transfer out afterwards if anything isn't going smoothly, then you must be happy if we deliver this baby in the vehicle. In that case, we'll pull over anyway and can open the back door and let Dell out.'

Harry's eyes flared. 'We're not delivering this baby in the ambulance. She should have gone to Alice Springs two days ago.'

'She wasn't in labour then. And you couldn't predict this.' Bonnie's voice was very quiet and very calm. 'And there's not a lot we can do about that now, Doctor.' She didn't look at him or he'd have known she was ready to throw something at him for the misplaced tension in his face. She knew that he had issues but at the moment that was just tough.

'I'll get the ambulance if you want to ring Alice Springs and arrange for someone to meet us half-way.'

Harry wasn't finished. 'This is a prime example of you providing another episode I don't want to be a part of.'

'Whoa there, cowboy.' Bonnie didn't fancy the sound of that. 'Like what, Harry?' She felt like poking him in the chest but restrained herself. One of them needed to. 'What else have I forced you into? A brief fling in Bali? I didn't see you running away. In fact, I'd say you did the chasing. And I certainly didn't force you to come here and confront maternal medicine. But you are here so confront it.'

He didn't like that. 'We don't have time for this.'

'No, we don't, but you started it, and I'll be finished before Steve gets here so you can darned well listen.' She brushed the hair out of her eyes and fixed her eyes on his.

'You can't go on like this, Harry. Fear doesn't have a part of caring for pregnant women.'

He lifted his head. 'And we should have shipped her out because I'm not sure I can lose that factor.'

Stubborn, more than anything, she thought. 'Or maybe you don't want to because that would mean you're moving on? Why is it so hard to let go of the fear and guilt, Harry?'

He shook his head. 'It's not fear, it's caution.'

She felt like saying that was piffle. But she didn't. She really couldn't be bothered getting childish. 'Caution is fine, but we're guardians who stand at the side of nature, not the directors. Women have been doing this longer than we've been interfering.'

'From my perspective I can't trust things not to go wrong. You can't deny the mortality rate has fallen since we did start to interfere.'

'We're not talking penicillin here, Harry.' Bonnie sighed. 'The last thing Tameeka needs

is a harbinger of doom draped around her neck.'
She breathed out heavily and then glanced at the
closed door to the consulting room.

'Doom happened to me. I can't forget that.'

'You told me you did everything possible. What
makes you think I don't understand? It's not a
new thing to lose a patient when the incident is
greater than the resources. You were there and
the resources weren't. Even in a major centre
most mothers still die with what your wife had.'

'If they say I was negligent, I think I'll believe
them.'

'I'm tempted to say "so what"? You hid away
in Bali believing that anyway. Even when you did
make a token return to medicine here in Ayers
Rock you have so many rules and safeguards
it's an escape anyway.' She shook her head and
glanced at her watch. 'I can't help your insecu-
rities but negative, fearful people should not be
around birthing women. Now I'm busy. Let's get
this girl to Alice Springs.'

Half an hour later they were thirty miles out of

the township as Bonnie drove into the magnificence of the fading light. The sun had finished posing to the masses and it wasn't a great time to be on the road with the wildlife coming out to feed at dusk but Harry obviously thought it more dangerous to have a normal birth than risk hitting a roo. Bonnie ground her teeth and concentrated on the road.

Harry was in the back, which was lucky for him because Bonnie had a mind to tell him a few more home truths. She had Bernie up front with her and she didn't want the poor guy to feel her frustration. He'd already backed down when Auntie Dell had said she'd get in the back.

The next half an hour saw two near misses of kangaroos and a lucky wombat, and Tameeka's noisy breathing from the back sounded like a freight train. Serves you right, Harry, Bonnie thought grimly. We could have been in a nice pleasant room back at the medical centre with electric lights and equipment if we needed it.

At the end of yet another half-hour, outside the

vehicle the light was restricted to the circular areas the headlights provided and the stars above. They still had an hour before they'd meet up with the other ambulance, and to make matters worse now a road train was bearing down on them from behind. Bonnie pulled over on a wide patch of dirt outside a rest area to let the monster truck go past.

'Bonnie?' Harry questioned from the back.

'I'm just letting the truck past.'

Then Tameeka's shaky voice. 'I gotta pee.'

Well, you can't wait another two hours, Bonnie thought silently, with a twitch of her lips. 'I'll just pull into this parking area.' Bonnie drove the few metres and reversed the vehicle so the back door was away from the road then turned the engine and headlights off. She jumped out and went around the back.

The night was quiet as the road train's engines faded into the distance and when she stepped away from the vehicle's cabin light the stars were brilliant and provided an amazing amount of gentle glow in the night sky.

Bernie was beside her and he lifted the back door up for her. Auntie Dell squeezed herself out like toothpaste from a tube and shook herself to stretch the bits that had been cramped in the back.

Then Harry helped Tameeka out and she leaned against Bernie when she could stand up. 'My back is killin' me when I lie down.'

'I know, sweetheart.' Bonnie looked around for some privacy for Tameeka. 'Come this way. I've got a torch in case we need it but there's some close scrub here, where you can go.'

'I don't need to do a wee,' Tameeka whispered. 'I just wanted to stop 'cause my back was killin' me.'

'That's okay.' Bonnie had her suspicions about the pressure the girl was getting now and wouldn't be surprised if this was it. 'You may as well go while you're here.'

Bonnie turned round to give her some privacy

and she could see Harry walking up and down beside the truck like an expectant father.

Tameeka groaned and when Bonnie turned round she was on all fours with her head down.

As soon as the pain eased, Bonnie helped her up. 'You push a little then, honey?'

'Mmm-hmm. And all that water came out. It's still comin' out. Don't make me get in that truck.'

'Let's just get back to the light.' This was it. Bonnie shrugged fatalistically. So be it.

Harry came towards them and Bonnie said quietly, 'Her waters broke. She's going to have the baby now and she doesn't want to get back in the ambulance. She wants to have it under the stars. Is that okay with you, Harry?'

Harry sighed, hugely, and she watched his tight shoulders finally drop with the breath. He lifted his head. 'It's all coming true, isn't it? The more I try to stop things happening, the more they seem to go against me. You were right. We would have been safer at the centre.' He smiled without humour.

He glanced ruefully up at the heavens. 'But it's not about me. It's about Tameeka. As long as we have emergency light when we need it, let's make it as good as we can for her. We'll get some blankets in case she needs to be lifted into the back in an emergency. There's four of us, we can lift her with the blanket.' They'd still needed contingency plans.

Then he smiled at her and Bonnie felt the tension slip from her shoulders like a huge sack of potatoes as Harry stopped fighting against her. She hadn't realised how much stress she'd been carrying around.

Thank goodness, Harry. Excellent man. About time.

They set up a little bed on the ground, and dimmed the back lights but left the front cabin light on.

Harry unobtrusively rubbed his forehead with two fingers and finally allowed the moment to soak in. He glanced across to where Auntie Dell sat cross-legged on the ground with Bernie hunched a handswidth away as Tameeka breathed quietly now in the still evening air.

The stars flickered and shone above like a carpet of guardian angels and somehow, with each of Tameeka's breaths, he could feel the pinpricks of pain that had burred into his skin for so long flicker and then fade away. Even more slowly he allowed Bonnie's words of earlier that day to sink in.

Tameeka was healthy, her baby had grown normally, and nothing had indicated there would be a problem. But he'd been determined to imagine every scenario that could go wrong.

He'd forced them onto the road and increased the risk when it would have been far safer to at least have facilities around them. He hadn't been smart, and his fear wasn't helpful to him, to the midwife and especially to the mother.

How far he'd come from the man who'd helped out at the birth centre in Ubud. How far from the joy and wonder he'd savoured with uncomplicated births just a few years ago.

Bonnie had tried to tell him that and he'd refused to listen. But still she sat with her hands clasped loosely in front of her. A towel lay across her lap, waiting to dry the baby.

She looked so calm, yet instantly attuned to every nuance of Tameeka's needs, and he envied her the faith he should have had, hoped he'd have again, thanks to nights like this and to Bonnie.

He'd had that faith once and after tonight he was determined to find it again. He'd lost the passion for well women doing what nature intended somewhere in his worry for himself.

Bonnie had sent him on the quest, and while it wasn't comfortable it had finally begun to feel right. This woman he'd been fated to meet, and who'd startled him out of his destructive stupor, shining brightly on the edge of his vision, then slowly lighting up his sky until she'd gradually warmed him from within.

She'd banished the darkness that even the brightness of Bali hadn't been able to penetrate.

Fifteen minutes later, with the night still

warm and bright, with little breeze and just as Tameeka's baby's head crowned, a brilliant shooting star shot across the horizon like a smiling angel. Harry felt the magic as he glanced across at Bonnie and counted himself doubly fortunate to be there.

Harry leant across and rested his hand on the small of Bonnie's back as she lifted the mewling infant to her mother's breast.

'Now, that's what I call birthin',' Auntie Dell said.

CHAPTER TEN

OF COURSE mother and baby were well and they called off the Alice Springs ambulance. Harry drove back to Uluru. A beaming Bernie sat in the back with his family.

Tameeka slept with her baby stretched across her chest like a kitten and her baby's father keeping watch over them both.

When Harry broke the silence, it wasn't awkward—nothing could be while they all floated in post-birth euphoria—but the events of the day lay between them, waiting for the time he had to speak. 'I've been hard work, Bonnie.'

'This sounds familiar.' He could hear the smile in her voice. 'Like another birth.'

'Good grief.' Harry looked across at her and he could feel his mouth tilt. 'I think we're actually forming a bit of history.'

She widened her eyes theatrically. 'Not the *H* word, Harry? Oh, my goodness.'

It was okay. She understood. He had the impression she would always understand. 'You were right. Tameeka's birth was amazing. She was incredible.'

'Yes, she was. I think I mentioned she's designed to do it.'

'Okay, Miss Smarty Pants, you may have. But let's keep the births for the centre in Alice next time.'

'Yes, Doctor.' Demurely. He'd like to kiss that respectability away but he'd have to wait. But he could plan.

That was when it hit him. Splat, like the yellow smear on the windshield in front of him, drawn to the light, followed by a short, sharp blow as life as he knew it was wiped out. He loved her.

He'd fallen in love. He'd said he couldn't do it again and she'd made him. He'd lost his heart when he'd vowed he'd never risk that again.

He'd thought he'd been attracted, get back on

the bike kind of attracted, which had drawn him here from Bali and suggested he needed to practise reconnecting with women without the drama of falling in love. Just rapport and teasing and maybe a little more of that lovely sex without strings.

But that hadn't happened. He was so stupid he could see it now like his own comet in the sky. That would be the comet that was going to wipe him out.

This was squeeze the heart, protect with your life, make babies and die together kind of falling in love—which was a whole different scenario and one he'd vowed never to be a part of ever, ever again.

He glanced out the window into the wall of darkness beside him and forcibly resisted the urge to slow the ambulance until it stopped, open the door and just walk away.

He was trapped. Trapped by his promise to Steve for another week, trapped by internal walls he'd trusted to protect him, trapped by the woman beside him who had crumbled those walls with her straight talking and straight looks that flew straight to his heart, and now he was in deep trouble.

He couldn't help it. He went into defence mode. Couldn't stop it. If she hated him, good. He needed distance for the next few days until he could get himself away.

'If it happens again, I'll ask for a different midwife.'

Bonnie blinked and the curve of her lips dropped with shock. He was joking. Wasn't he? Her head swivelled to look at him and he was staring straight ahead with his mouth a grim line and cheeks stiff and stark in the reflected light. He wasn't joking. 'What did you just say?'

'I won't have my patients put at risk again. All pregnant women will be in Alice Springs a month before they're due.'

Bonnie's mind raced. What the heck had happened in the space of a minute? 'Certainly,

Doctor. Perhaps we should send them when their pregnancy tests come up positive. At ten weeks.'

The stranger said, 'I don't want to discuss it any more. You know how I feel.'

Bonnie shook her head, still reeling but very close to telling him where to go. 'I know how the other doctor who was here five minutes ago felt, but this new guy is a pain.'

She would have said more, hadn't even started on what she felt like saying, but another road train had stopped at the side of the road and the driver waved them down.

Good. Anything to get her mind off the slow death she was planning for Harry.

Harry was pleased at the distraction too. He wasn't happy with the option his brain had chosen—to alienate Bonnie—but he guessed it had worked. She looked ready to jump out of the car herself.

This day was never going to end. He slowed and pulled up beside the truck driver as Bonnie wound down her window.

'You okay?' she asked, but he could see the man was holding his right arm tightly across his chest.

Trouble was confirmed when the man said, 'Got me fingers caught in the cattle gate.' He grimaced. 'Doesn't feel right.'

'Let's see.' Harry climbed out and Bonnie opened her door to get the bandages from the back, he guessed. Dell and Bernie climbed out and Harry could hear her rummaging through the drawers for the first-aid supplies.

By the time she'd returned to the truck driver Harry had him sitting on a log and was ready to bind the fingers.

He pretended to the world that everything was normal. He pretended to himself. 'Bonnie, this is Blue.'

Typically, Blue had a thatch of bright red hair that glowed even in the dark. His name was standard country humour about redheads, probably his nickname since school days.

Blue was in pain, Harry could see that, because

his plastering of freckles stood out starkly across his nose and his pale face. Maybe not too much pain because his eyes lit up when he saw Bonnie, and Harry felt himself frown.

'G'day, there, Bonnie, you're a sight for sore eyes,' Blue drawled. He tipped his Akubra and the twinkle in his eyes was unmistakable. Blue was a larrikin, no doubt about it, and Bonnie didn't seem to mind.

Bonnie smiled at the man in a way that seemed just a little too friendly and made Harry realise just how far he'd sunk.

'Hello, there, Blue. Nice to meet you,' she said. 'I'll bet your fingers throb like blazes.'

Harry cut her off. 'Looks like you've broken two, and damaged the thumb badly.' He glanced at Blue's pale face, 'Lucky you didn't chop them off, judging by the slice here.'

Blue nodded, distracted from Bonnie, Harry was pleased to see, and much less amused. 'Yeah. Thought I did, happy to count 'em after I got 'em out of the gate.' He shrugged. 'At least the cattle didn't get out. One of the bolts worked loose and I'd fixed that first—bloody lucky—before I stuffed meself.'

Harry made short work of stabilising and binding Blue's fingers and then looked up at the truck. 'You'll need X-rays and suturing at the clinic at Uluru, we're the closest. Can you squeeze in the back with the others?'

Blue looked doubtfully at the ambulance and then at his truck. Harry correctly interpreted his concern. 'Sorry, I can't drive your rig. Can you phone someone to help?'

Blue scratched his head with his good hand. 'Might take a day or two and the cattle need to get to the sales.'

Bonnie stepped between them. 'If you sit in the cab with me, Blue, I can drive you to the medical centre, then you could take over once the doctor's fixed you up.' Bonnie turned her shoulder away from Harry to face the injured man and Harry saw Blue's eyes widen even further in admiration. Harry didn't miss that.

She went on, 'I worked out at Kununurra and drove a rig like this from Halls Creek six months ago when the driver had chest pain and we couldn't get help.' She glanced dismissively at Harry. 'The doctor has the ambulance covered.'

Of course she could drive a truck with three trailers on a dirt road. He probably could too, if he wanted to. She and Blue would have a lovely time. Harry felt like swearing but refrained. At least the man was injured. And he had no right to even think like that.

'You go ahead, Doctor,' Bonnie said firmly.

It was all good. He'd get space to get his head around how he was going to get out of Uluru without Bonnie finding out. And he'd bet Blue would look after her. Harry dug his toe into the dirt and then flicked a rock out towards the grass. It was great she could drive the rig. Really.

'Let's load up, then.' Harry glanced at Bernie, who obediently jumped into the back, and Dell paused as she surveyed the empty passenger seat.

'I'll come and sit beside you then, Doc.' Auntie Dell was happy. 'I reckon that'll be real comfy.'

'Lovely,' Harry said through his teeth. They all climbed in and Harry started the ambulance.

'Ya know…' Auntie Dell had been thinking. 'You and her should start a birth place for the women around here, Doc. Them girls don't wanna go away from their families to have their babies.'

Harry almost laughed out loud at the simplistic concept. 'It's a bit more complicated than that.'

'Nothing complicated about having a baby. It's getting the girls five hours' drive away at the right time that's complicated.'

The next day, Bonnie saw very little of Harry. If she entered a room he exited unless it was medically impossible, and at those times they were both too busy to worry about anything.

Even when Leila, the little girl they'd met at the Rock that first morning, came in with her mother and Auntie Dell with a nasty dose of gastro, Harry had eyes only for the toddler, and the way he cajoled the little one to a smile made the difference in his attitude to her even more noticeable, at least to Bonnie.

He stroked the child's fine hair as he looked at Shay. 'You might need to take Leila to the hospital at Alice Springs.' He shook his head at Leila's slightly sunken eyes and dull skin and erred on the side of caution, as usual.

Shay cast an agonised glance at Auntie Dell, who cast one at Bonnie—who suppressed a sigh. She was almost over going in to bat for everyone else.

That was what happened when a workplace lost equality between professionals. This was all Harry's fault. If she didn't know better, or try to believe better anyway, she'd say he was being as difficult as he possibly could just to incense her.

They both knew it was hard for the women to get to Alice Springs and how unpleasant the journey would be with a sick child. Leila wasn't quite sick enough for the Flying Doctor to pick up and really just needed a watchful eye and some IV fluids.

'Shay wondered if we could try with IV fluids here,' Bonnie said steadily. 'Through today anyway. And see if Leila improves.' She glanced away from Harry's expressionless face to the mother, whom she smiled at to relieve the tension. 'Because that's what children can do.'

Shay smiled back with relief and Bonnie added, 'Then Leila could go home and get checked again in the morning.'

At least Harry considered it. 'And if she gets worse?'

'You'd check her before she went home and, of course, Shay would bring her back during the night if she was worried, wouldn't you, Shay?'

Shay nodded vigorously and Auntie Dell nodded once, firmly. Come on, Harry, Bonnie thought with a sigh. The little one is sick, but not critical, and was even starting to improve in front of their eyes. They could handle this here for the moment and maybe the family wouldn't have to be thrown into upheaval.

Thankfully he seemed to listen to her for a change, and even snap out of his mode enough to agree, albeit grudgingly. 'I'll check her later and decide then. Before three o'clock.'

Good. Bonnie threw in for good measure, 'Shay's Tameeka's older sister.'

'Really?' Harry's face twitched into a smile she didn't expect. 'How's Tameeka doing with her baby?' Harry asked.

'Real good,' Auntie Dell answered for her niece with a big white grin. 'Bernie's telling everyone how amazin' that birth was.'

'Great,' Harry said, and glanced at Bonnie. 'Hope we aren't going to have a rush of last-minute labours.'

Bonnie smiled grimly to herself. She'd asked for that. But he had seemed in a better mood. Though it was easier to hate him when he was a pain. Nice Harry was too hard to ignore.

She kept Leila until late in the afternoon, when,

with the resilience of children and the extra fluids they'd infused, the little girl was ready to go home with her mum and Auntie Dell.

'I'll just get the doctor to check her one more time, Shay.'

Leila's mother nodded and Bonnie tracked Harry down in the records room, checking statistics. They looked like antenatal ones. Now what was his problem?

'Can you see Leila now, please? She looks much improved.'

He nodded and followed her out to the main assessment room. The little girl even smiled at him and Bonnie felt the tug of her heart at Harry's rapport with the little one.

'You were right, Bonnie,' he said after they left. 'She didn't need to go.'

He offered her a strangely whimsical smile she didn't know how to react to. 'I want to finish what I'm doing tonight and then I have something to show you. Probably tomorrow.'

He paused, then added, 'You'll be glad when

I'm gone and a reasonable doctor arrives that you can work with.' He didn't give her a chance to answer, just walked away, and Bonnie shook her head. Her heart might not agree but it was getting that way.

The next morning Bonnie felt unwell. She must have caught the bug Leila had because the thought of breakfast was not a pleasant one.

Her face paled and she rushed for the bathroom. Obviously the thought was enough.

Afterwards she fell back on her bed and wiped her face with the washer she'd grabbed from the sink. Whew. At least she felt a little better now.

She reached across to the night table and picked up the phone to ring Vicki and let her know she'd be late when someone knocked on the door. She groaned. She hoped it wasn't Harry. Today was not a good day.

'Go away,' she muttered into the empty room. The person knocked again and she sighed as she sat up gingerly and finally made her way over to the door.

She leant her head on the edge of the door as it opened. 'Not this morning, Harry. Not well.'

'What's wrong?'

'Haven't searched for a diagnosis, Doctor,' she said faintly, 'but I'm guessing I caught Leila's bug.'

'You look like death. Back to bed.' He pushed her back into the room gently and pulled back her covers. 'In you go.' She climbed in and he tucked her up like Gran used to do. Thankfully there was no sign of the grumpy doctor at all, and it felt weepily good.

When her head hit the pillow she closed her eyes, but she could hear a rattle in the corner of the room and Harry reappeared with the metal wastepaper bin and a glass of water. 'Just in case.'

He grimaced in sympathy. 'Sip water. I'll be back in a while to check on you. I'll bring some lemonade or something.'

Bonnie heard the door close quietly and she sighed. At least she didn't have to try to go to work. She felt rotten.

By ten o'clock she felt fine. 'Shortest bug in history,' she said to Vicki when she walked in.

Harry's consulting-room door opened for him to show out a patient and he stopped when he saw her. 'What're you doing here?'

'I've recovered and I'm bored.'

Harry looked at his watch. 'It's morning tea time for me. Fancy some food, then?' He was looking at her strangely and she frowned at him.

'Only if you want some.'

His frown was heavy. 'I think so.'

He was acting oddly. Just an uneasy prickling that made her look at Vicki with a lift of her brows. Vicki shrugged in silent reply, as if to say, 'I don't know what's up with him.'

Bonnie had no choice but to duck under his arm as he held the door open for her.

'It's too far to the coffee shop. How about a cup of tea in the dining room?'

'Okay.' This was getting stranger by the minute.

He ushered her into the deserted dining room and plugged in the kettle. Then he sat her down.

'Steve's found a replacement for me and he flies in tomorrow. I fly out in the evening.'

Bonnie bit her lip. She hated fighting with him but she wasn't sure she wanted him to go. In fact, she was darned sure she didn't want him to go, which was weird when he drove her insane.

'Where are you going?'

'I'm heading to Katherine to finish something I should have finished a long time ago. Then I'm going on to Darwin. I'm meeting a few people who are interested in a proposal I might have.'

'That sounds good, Harry. Vague, but I'm glad for you.'

Then he said something totally off topic. 'It's five weeks since you left Bali.'

Time flew. Or did it? It felt like a year. 'So?'

He was peering at her. 'You were nauseated this morning.'

Horribly so. His point was? 'And?'

'Aren't you suspicious?'

'I'm getting a bit suspicious of you. Have you been drinking, Harry?'

'This isn't a joke.

'Okay, Harry. Enough guessing games. Yes, I was sick this morning. What of it, Harry? Maybe I didn't wash my hands well enough after looking after Leila?'

'Come on, Bonnie. You're a midwife.'

Bonnie blinked. 'What…?' Then it dawned on her what he was talking about. 'Don't be ridiculous. No! One time.' She shook her head. 'I have one word for you. Protection. That's why they call it that.'

She shook her head at his presumption. 'I thought you had tickets on yourself the first time I saw you.'

He glanced down at the floor and if she wasn't mistaken she'd almost think he was disappointed. Good grief.

But when he looked up his eyes were sharp again. 'Then you've had a period since Bali?'

Now she was getting angry. And just a little worried as she calculated madly. 'Spare me. You may be a doctor but you're not my doctor.'

She stood up. 'Have a good flight tomorrow, Harry. If I don't see you, that will be good.'

Harry watched her walk away. Well, that hadn't gone well. Understatement. He'd been sitting in his office before his last patient when it had hit him. And nothing could *un*convince him that was why she was sick. He didn't know why he was so positively certain. He'd checked dates, they worked out. He'd checked the net, it was unlucky but possible, and all he'd need to do was find out if she knew.

She didn't but he still didn't rule the possibility out. And the really strange thing was, now that the absolute worst that could have happened might have happened, he actually felt euphoric.

It was ridiculous but curiously liberating. There was no use running away. If it had happened. And actually worked with his new plans, as long as she'd have him.

If he was lucky, he was going to have to watch a woman he loved go through a pregnancy and he would have to conquer his fear. As Bonnie was fond of saying, he had to trust Mother Nature.

Because he wanted to be there. Wanted to see every change, be a part of every new experience, see the things he'd missed out on last time, be there for the normal birth that he would have to learn to trust in. The birth of Bonnie's baby, and his.

Now all he had to do was convince her he was a sane and sensible man, which could be difficult given his behaviour over the last few weeks.

CHAPTER ELEVEN

BONNIE escaped to her room, steering down the empty hallway like a remote-controlled car, not sure who was driving while her mind raced.

She pushed open the door and pulled it shut behind her back. When she leant against it the wood was the only cool thing on her body. She stared at her pale face in the mirror on the wall and slowly closed her eyes.

Her fingers inched reluctantly down until she rested them over her pelvic bone. She was pregnant. No period, nausea, slight tenderness when she'd put her bra on that morning. Good grief.

How the heck had this happened and how could she not be absolutely devastated? Well, she knew how it happened but the lack of a sense of impending doom surprised her. Because it wasn't there. She was stunned and shocked but below those initial layers of disbelief lurked a tiny secret whisper of joy.

She was having Harry's baby.

And in the absolutely worst-case scenario she could tell her baby she'd loved its daddy.

Therapeutic, in fact, to admit it. Accept the truth of it. Stop denying the truth. She loved annoying, frustrating, gorgeous Harry with every cell in her body. And now she was sharing cells with him as they created their baby.

And if she'd gathered Harry's reaction correctly, he wasn't devastated either. Which opened up a whole new amazing realm of possibility.

When Harry knocked on her door three minutes later she opened her eyes. She knew it was him. Could feel the awareness through an inch of wood. They certainly had some talking to do.

She opened the door and he stood there tall and almost relaxed, which was a first since he'd arrived in the centre. She lifted her brows. When he smiled at her it held all the light and brightness and excitement she associated with the man she'd met in Bali.

Drat the man. He had too many good angles that made her forget how much he could drive her mad. These were all reasons he could sweep her off her feet but it was the question behind his eyes that really clinched it for her.

The wonder of his new self-knowledge, the warmth of a man who could feel complete with the woman he loved—and wanted her to feel the same.

'I've brought you a gift.' He held open his hand and the little silver baby he'd given her in Bali lay in his palm. 'I'd really love you to keep this.' He looked at her. 'Along with my heart.'

She knew she loved him, had done so since that magical night at his house in Bali, but he didn't deserve things to be easy. 'Do I have your heart, Harry?'

'If you let me in, I could try to convince you.'

They were married at sunset on top of a red sand dune overlooking the Rock. A wedding dune, with white Balinese flags flying in a circle. Bernie was on the didgeridoo, playing haunting Aboriginal music, with a little dark-eyed girl in a white dress dropping white rose petals Harry had had flown in from Victoria.

Harry had flown down Bonnie's friends from Darwin and his colleagues from the RFDS had done a fly-past with white ribbons in the sky.

The bride and groom exchanged solemn vows, eyes only for each other as they held hands, and Steve as celebrant, pronounced them man and wife. Later there would be another wedding in Ubud and another circle of friends would be there.

When the stars came out the astronomer from the Sounds of Silence Dinner wove dreamtime stories of ancient love between planets, myths of romance and the Greek gods, astrology and the attraction of opposite star signs, and Harry and Bonnie smiled at each other as they watched their guests' rapt faces.

'We need to do this once a year for our anniversary,' Bonnie whispered. 'I love learning about the stars and listening to the stories.'

'And I love listening to you,' Harry teased. 'Even when I'm in trouble.'

Seven months later

Their car drew up outside the Uluru Birthing Centre. Bonnie breathed out the last of her contraction and put her hand on Harry's arm. 'Sacha can catch our baby.'

Harry looked across. 'I'll catch our baby.'

Bonnie raised her eyebrows. 'And how are you going to do that and hold my hand at the same time?'

'One-handed.'

Bonnie began to breathe as the next contraction built. 'Harry, I need your hand.'

Harry smiled at this woman he adored more than life itself. 'Sacha can catch our baby, my love. I knew your caseload midwifery would do me out of catching babies.'

'You don't really mind.'

He leant across and kissed her brow. 'I'll be the husband. I get the easy job. Have I told you lately that I love you?'

The pain eased and Bonnie sighed as she prepared herself mentally to stand up. 'Not in the last half an hour.'

'Sorry.' Harry leant across and kissed her lips gently. 'I love you.' He opened his door. 'Wait. I'll help you.'

She watched him climb out fast but still with that effortless grace he'd always had. 'I love you too,' she said to the empty car, and smiled.

* * * * *

January

THE PLAYBOY OF HARLEY STREET	Anne Fraser
DOCTOR ON THE RED CARPET	Anne Fraser
JUST ONE LAST NIGHT...	Amy Andrews
SUDDENLY SINGLE SOPHIE	Leonie Knight
THE DOCTOR & THE RUNAWAY HEIRESS	Marion Lennox
THE SURGEON SHE NEVER FORGOT	Melanie Milburne

February

CAREER GIRL IN THE COUNTRY	Fiona Lowe
THE DOCTOR'S REASON TO STAY	Dianne Drake
WEDDING ON THE BABY WARD	Lucy Clark
SPECIAL CARE BABY MIRACLE	Lucy Clark
THE TORTURED REBEL	Alison Roberts
DATING DR DELICIOUS	Laura Iding

March

CORT MASON – DR DELECTABLE	Carol Marinelli
SURVIVAL GUIDE TO DATING YOUR BOSS	Fiona McArthur
RETURN OF THE MAVERICK	Sue MacKay
IT STARTED WITH A PREGNANCY	Scarlet Wilson
ITALIAN DOCTOR, NO STRINGS ATTACHED	Kate Hardy
MIRACLE TIMES TWO	Josie Metcalfe

Mills & Boon® Large Print Medical

April

BREAKING HER NO-DATES RULE	Emily Forbes
WAKING UP WITH DR OFF-LIMITS	Amy Andrews
TEMPTED BY DR DAISY	Caroline Anderson
THE FIANCÉE HE CAN'T FORGET	Caroline Anderson
A COTSWOLD CHRISTMAS BRIDE	Joanna Neil
ALL SHE WANTS FOR CHRISTMAS	Annie Claydon

May

THE CHILD WHO RESCUED CHRISTMAS	Jessica Matthews
FIREFIGHTER WITH A FROZEN HEART	Dianne Drake
MISTLETOE, MIDWIFE...MIRACLE BABY	Anne Fraser
HOW TO SAVE A MARRIAGE IN A MILLION	Leonie Knight
SWALLOWBROOK'S WINTER BRIDE	Abigail Gordon
DYNAMITE DOC OR CHRISTMAS DAD?	Marion Lennox

June

NEW DOC IN TOWN	Meredith Webber
ORPHAN UNDER THE CHRISTMAS TREE	Meredith Webber
THE NIGHT BEFORE CHRISTMAS	Alison Roberts
ONCE A GOOD GIRL...	Wendy S. Marcus
SURGEON IN A WEDDING DRESS	Sue MacKay
THE BOY WHO MADE THEM LOVE AGAIN	Scarlet Wilson